Jacky could feel the surgeon's hand under her elbow as he propelled her up the wide, sweeping oak staircase to the upper floor. There was a faint odour of expensive after-shave emanating from somewhere above her head, and the combination of Dr Harvey's overpowering personality and the opulence of the estate had rendered her temporarily speechless. She mumbled something about her first impression being one of exceptional beauty.

He paused on the stairs and turned towards her. 'First impressions are always important,' he agreed, and looking up, she saw that his dark brown eyes held an earnest, enigmatic expression. She felt a shiver of apprehension run down her spine and wondered if he knew who she really was. No, that's impossible, she told herself as she turned away and began to mount the stairs alone. I would never have got the job if he'd known.

Margaret Barker pursued a variety of interesting careers before she became a full-time author. Besides holding a BA degree in French and Linguistics she is a Licentiate of the Royal Academy of Music, a State Registered Nurse and a qualified teacher. Whilst living in Africa Margaret had a radio programme with the Nigerian Broadcasting Corporation. Happily married for more that thirty years, she has two sons, a daughter and three grandchildren. Her travels in Europe, Asia, Africa and America have given Margaret the background for her foreign novels and the teaching hospital in England where she trained has provided ideas for her medical romances. She lives with her husband in a sixteenth century thatched house near the sea.

Surgeon Royal is Margaret Barker's tenth Doctor Nurse Romance. Recent titles include *Anatomy of Love, Monsoon Surgeon* and *Doctor in the Dales*.

SURGEON ROYAL

BY

MARGARET BARKER

MILLS & BOON LIMITED
ETON HOUSE   18-24 PARADISE ROAD
RICHMOND   SURREY   TW9 1SR

First published in Great Britain 1988
by Mills & Boon Limited

© Margaret Barker 1988

Australian copyright 1988
Philippine copyright 1988
This edition 1988

ISBN 0 263 76278 5

Set in Times 10 on 10½ pt.
03 – 8811 – 49,933

Typeset in Great Britain by JCL Graphics, Bristol

Made and printed in Great Britain

CHAPTER ONE

DR CARL HARVEY was not what Jacky had expected. She had hated him for so long that she had built up a mental picture of a grotesque unapproachable creature, devoid of all feelings. But now, face to face with this tall, handsome, smiling stranger, she felt herself go weak at the knees. Could this really be the man who had been responsible for her boyfriend's death? The question hammered in her brain as she accepted the outstretched hand. Firm fingers closed round hers and she experienced a frisson of guilt and fear; guilt at the subterfuge she had used to land herself in this plum medical assignment and fear of what might happen if the eminent surgeon discovered her involvement with Chris.

'How was your journey, Sister Diamond?' Brown eyes set in a strong, classically featured face stared down at her. He was still holding on to her hand and she was afraid he would feel her trembling. Perhaps he'll put it down to nerves, she hoped. It is, after all, a very important, not to mention prestigious job. She forced herself to meet his gaze without flinching.

'There were no problems with the flight from London, but it took a long time to get through Immigration here in Detroit,' she answered coolly.

'That's only to be expected when you're working for the royal family of Reichenstein. You'll get used to it,' he told her easily.

'This is my first experience of royalty at close quarters,' Jacky admitted, encouraged by the warmth of his smile.

He laughed, and once again she wondered how such

an evil man could be so pleasant. In fact he was more
than pleasant. If she hadn't hated him so much she
would have found him positively attractive, especially
when he laughed and displayed those fabulous white
teeth.

'There's no need to worry about Prince George,' the
surgeon assured her. 'I was at school with him in
England and he's not a bit stuffy. He won't stand on
ceremony except on public occasions when it's expected
of him. And his wife, Princess Karine, is delightful.
Let's go inside and meet them.'

He turned and began to climb the wide stone steps in
front of the large majestic mansion. As Jacky followed
the tall debonair figure in the immaculate grey suit she
noticed that her luggage had been whisked away by a
couple of white-coated stewards. The huge, luxurious
limousine that had met her at the airport had purred
away from the ornate gardens to some nether region
where, no doubt, it would be polished back to pristine
condition. She gave an involuntary sigh as she passed
through the wide open oak door into a magnificent
panelled hall of vast proportions. It was going to be
quite an experience living in a place like this!

'The old auto barons did themselves proud,'
whispered Carl Harvey with a boyish grin, going on to
explain that the mansion had belonged to the family of
one of the automative 'royalty' who had made their
fortune when Detroit became the motor capital of the
world. 'Many of these historic homes have become
museums, but the Prince was lucky enough to be able to
take a lease on this one for the duration of his visit to
the United States. What do you think of it?'

Jacky could feel the surgeon's hand under her elbow
as he propelled her up the wide, sweeping oak staircase
to the upper floor. There was a faint odour of expensive
after-shave emanating from somewhere above her head,
and the combination of Dr Harvey's overpowering

personality and the opulence of the estate had rendered her temporarily speechless. She mumbled somthing about her first impression being one of exceptional beauty.

He paused on the stairs and turned towards her. 'First impressions are always important,' he agreed, and looking up, she saw that his dark brown eyes held an earnest, enigmatic expression. She felt a shiver of apprehension run down her spine and wondered if he knew who she really was. No, that's impossible, she told herself as she turned away and began to mount the stairs alone. I would never have got the job if he'd known.

He was right behind her as they reached the gallery.

'The Prince is expecting us in his study,' he explained, tapping lightly on an ornately carved door.

It was opened after a few seconds by a young fresh-faced secretary who smiled as she recognised the surgeon.

'Come in, Dr Harvey,' she said in a clipped, mid-European accent, before returning to her desk in a corner of the large room.

The Prince rose from his chair by the wide leaded lighted casement windows and came across the room to greet them.

'So this is the charming young Sister who is to help you with your medical work, Carl. How do you do?' He held out his hand and grasped hers firmly.

'How do you do, sir?' Jacky replied nervously wondering if she should have said "sire' or maybe 'Your Highness'. Oh well, Dr Harvey had told her the Prince only stood on ceremony on public occasions, she figured. And this could hardly be called a public occasion, but still it would be nice to know . . .

'Have you seen your quarters?' the Prince asked briskly.

'No, not yet . . .' she began.

'We came straight up here to see you, George . . .'

Oh, so it was all right for her boss to be on intimate terms, she noticed, but she doubted if the same courtesy would be extended to her! The two men were, after all, old school chums. She heard the surgeon explaining that Madeleine was going to take care of all that. Who on earth was Madeleine?

As if the lady in question had read her thoughts there was another tap on the door and a tall, elegant, ageless creature was ushered in. She could have been any age between thirty and forty-five, but Jacky guessed she must be in her late thirties. But she had a timeless quality that denoted either hours spent in the beauty shop or an exceptionally healthy constitution. Jacky noted the long, tapering fingernails, the immaculate blonde hair framing a perfectly made up face.

'This is my secretary, Madeleine Cummings; Sister Jacky Diamond.'

Jacky drew in her breath as the surgeon made the introductions. My God, she thought anxiously, I never thought he'd bring his secretary with him from England! But then, on second thoughts, why ever not? The woman is so efficient she must be completely indispensable. She remembered the numerous occasions when she had tried to contact the great man himself, only to be told by Ms Cummings that 'Dr Harvey is in conference' or 'I'm afraid the surgeon is unavailable today. If you would care to put your request in writing . . .' Well, she'd tried writing, hadn't she, and a fat lot of good it had done her . . .

'I'll show you to your room, Sister,' murmured the paragon with a polite smile.

Jacky gritted her teeth and prepared to follow.

'Do rest before this evening,' Dr Harvey advised her in a smooth bedside-manner voice. 'We're going to escort Prince George to an important dinner, so you'd better not be suffering from jet-lag.'

'Will you require my services this evening, Carl?' his

secretary asked demurely.

'I think not. Take the night off . . .' Dr Harvey began, but Ms Cummings interrupted him.

'I'll catch up on that backlog of correspondence. And now, if you're ready, Sister?'

Easy to see who takes care of the administration here, thought Jacky wryly. And everything else, I shouldn't wonder. There was an easygoing relationship between the surgeon and his secretary. It must surely spill over into their personal life. She glanced at the Prince, thinking, inconsequentially, that he was remarkably unprepossessing for a royal personage with his average stature and short-cropped sandy hair. If she had been asked to pick out the Prince from the two men in front of her she would most definitely have pointed out the distinguished-looking Dr Carl Harvey. How deceptive looks can be! she thought as she followed the secretary out of the study.

Her bedroom was on the next floor at the end of a long corridor carpeted with some kind of antique Indian carpet. A bowl of fragrant roses had been placed on a low table by the window. Jacky crossed the room quickly to admire the view. As she hoped, the room looked out across Lake St. Clair towards the Canadian shore. A light summer breeze had whipped up white flecks on the grey water. She watched, fascinated, as a large blue and white passenger ship emerged from the Detroit River and made its way across the lake. For a few moments she forgot her hostility towards the surgeon.

'What a beautiful view!' she breathed.

'Yes, isn't it?' Madeleine Cummings joined her at the window.

The aroma of French perfume brought Jacky back to reality and she looked at the woman by her side. 'Have you worked for Dr Harvey for very long?' she asked boldly.

The secretary gave a short tinkling laugh. 'You're not going to find out my age as easily as you think,' was her disarming reply.

'Nothing was further from my mind,' stuttered Jacky.

'You'd be surprised at the way people try to worm things out of you. I've worked for Dr Harvey longer than I care to remember, but that doesn't mean I've got one foot in the grave,' Ms Cummings continued calmly. 'Admittedly, I won't see thirty again.'

The woman must have some sort of hang-up about her age, Jacky thought in exasperation. I wish she'd go away and leave me in peace! An over whelming feeling of weariness was stealing over her. Must be the jet-lag the doctor warned me about, she decided.

'Thank you for showing me up here,' she told the secretary, adding in a firm voice that she planned to take a nap.

'Good idea,' the older woman agreed, taking the hint and making for the door. 'You're going to need all your strength in this job. I hope you didn't think it was a soft option from hospital life. It's going to be no holiday.'

'I never imagined it would be.' Jacky stared after the departing figure before she went over and locked the door firmly. Leaning against it, she gave a sigh of relief as she took in her luxurious surroundings. The afternoon sun drifted through the casement windows, bringing out the rich ruby red colour of the thick carpet. The curtains, a perfect match, were held back with gold satin bands to allow maximum sunlight to filter through. There was something chaste about the white lace of the counterpane, Jacky decided. Yes, it was definitely a virginal kind of room. Perhaps it had been used by an auto baron's daughter before her marriage. There were delicate porcelain ornaments on the oak mantelpiece; one was a lady in a crinoline and there were several tiny animals. The fireplace looked as if it was no longer used; a large earthenware vase of lilies had been placed in the centre.

Obviously the room has been well cared for, she thought as she crossed to the door that led into her bathroom. There must be an army of servants to look after the place! Let's hope they're all healthy and don't need any medical attention while I have my bath.

The hot water gushed out of the antique brass taps as she lay back in the scented foam. Bliss! she told herself, wiggling her toes among the bubbles. I've only ever seen a huge bath like this with such enormous taps in a stately castle in England, one day when it was open to the public. I could almost swim in this one!

After such a pleasurable experience it wasn't difficult to drift off to sleep between the cool sheets. By the time Jacky woke up the sun was low in the sky and the room had a distinct evening chill. She glanced at the bedside phone, which had remained blessedly silent during her siesta, but which was now emitting a discreet purring noise. She reached for the handset, reflecting that even the telephone sounded regal.

'I need your assistance, Sister.'

She recognised Dr Harvey's deep virile tones immediately. 'Is anything wrong, sir?' she asked, sitting bolt upright amid the expensive bedlinen as she tried to gather her thoughts.

'I'd rather not discuss it on the phone. Get down here at once,' was the brusque reply.

'Where are . . .?' she began, but he cut in impatiently.

'In the medical wing—ground floor.'

The phone went dead, and Jacky stared into the earpiece as if expecting the tyrannical doctor to continue his abrupt orders.

'Yes, sir,' she whispered to the empty room, feeling almost a sense of relief that the surgeon was already showing his true colours. This was more like the man she had expected to meet! The suave debonair stranger she had seen a couple of hours ago had merely been putting on a façade to lull her into a false sense of security. She had been slightly taken in by his performance, but not any more!

Her white uniform dress and crisp white cap lay at the top of her case, and she thanked her lucky stars that she had put them there for just such an emergency. Even so, it was five minutes before she was fully dressed and heading off down the corridor. There was not a trace of make-up on her face, but she didn't care. For any other man in the world Jacky Diamond would at least have put on a dash of lipstick, but Carl Harvey didn't deserve such consideration, in her estimation. She would do her job to the best of her ability, but there was to be nothing other than a distant professional relationship between herself and her new boss.

He was waiting for her in the entrance hall of the well-equipped medical wing, tapping his fingers impatiently on the polished woodwork of a nineteenth-century carved oak table.

'So glad you could make it,' he drawled sarcastically, glancing up at the hands of the ornate wall clock.

'I had to put my uniform on,' Jacky countered, but he had turned on his heel and was striding towards the swing doors that led into the inner sanctum of the medical rooms.

Fuming inwardly, Jacky followed the tall figure. He towered above her as he held back one of the doors. Glancing at his anxious face, she wondered what the emergency was and whether she would find it difficult to work with a doctor she disliked so much.

The doors led into a wide airy room which looked for all the world like the outpatients department of a small private hospital.

'In here,' the surgeon told her unceremoniously, and she followed him into a small consulting room. He motioned to her to take a chair before he sank down behind his desk. The distinctive smell of rich leather enveloped her as she waited quietly for her boss to speak.

He took his time, seemingly searching for the right

words as his deep brown eyes watched her face.

'Can I trust you?' he asked suddenly, and Jacky's heart missed a beat.

He knows! she thought. He's been discussing me with his secretary and they've sussed out who I am . . .

'Because if I can't then you're going to be no good to me in this job,' he continued without waiting for her reply. 'You must give me your assurance that you will never betray the confidence of our employers.'

'It goes without saying,' she assured him, feeling relieved that his concern was of a professional nature. She could breathe again!

'Princess Karine has asked me to examine her . . .' he paused and ran his fingers through his black hair, eyes still intent on her face. 'She suspects that she's pregnant.'

'But that's wonderful—isn't it?' Jacky added, realising that Dr Harvey looked anything but pleased. 'What's the problem?'

'The problem is that she wants the pregnancy—if there is one—to be a closely guarded secret,' replied the surgeon with an air of exasperation. 'No one must know—not even her husband.'

'Isn't that going to be a little difficult, sir?' she put in quietly, unable to conceal the smile of amusement that played on her lips. 'I mean, these things have a way of . . . er . . . revealing themselves.'

'This is not a joke,' he snapped, and then modifying his abrupt tone he continued with his explanation. 'Let me outline the medical case history. Princess Karine's first two pregnancies were normal and resulted in the births of Princess Charlotte, now eight, and Princess Helen, now six. Since her second confinement the Princess has suffered two miscarriages, both of them around the third month. She told me that this caused her great distress not only physically but mentally. The people of Reichenstein had already been alerted by the press and the media that there was possibility of a male heir to the throne, and her miscarriages took place in a glare of publicity, as you can imagine . . .'

'Poor woman!' breathed Jacky as she remembered the agony of some of her patients who had miscarried. 'It must have been dreadful to suffer like that and to be in the public eye.'

The surgeon relaxed his cool professional manner when he saw the sympathetic expression in her blue eyes. 'The Prince, too, was deeply affected and told his wife that he couldn't bear to see her suffer like that again. They consulted the royal gynaecologist and it was decided that the Princess should go on the pill. But some time ago she secretly decided that she wanted to have one last try for another baby, so she stopped taking it.'

'When did she tell you all this?' Jacky asked in an enthralled voice.

'Soon after you arrived,' he replied quietly. 'She sent for me and swore me to secrecy. Apparently she believes herself to be about three months and therefore around the danger point. I agreed to examine her this evening, and you're to be the only other person in on the secret apart from her devoted maid, Louise, who has been with the Princess's family since the Princess herself was a child.'

'But what about the Prince? He'll have to be told soon.' Jacky sat forward at the front of the wide leather chair and stared at the surgeon with perplexed eyes.

'Of course he'll be told—but not yet. The Princess was adamant that he should know nothing about it until the pregnancy is more advanced. She still fears that she's going to miscarry. That's why she sent for me today. She's worried about attending the dinner this evening. It's on a cruise liner which will sail on Lake St. Clair and there'll be dancing on board after dinner. She's afraid the excitement might prove too much for her in her delicate condition . . . That will be the Princess arriving now.' Dr Harvey jumped to his feet at the sound of voices and hurried over to open the door.

Jacky followed him and stood back to allow a slender dark-haired woman to enter the room. She was of medium height with tiny features that became attractive when she smiled. The older lady hovering behind her must be Louise, her maid, Jacky decided. She looked decidedly annoyed when her mistress dismissed her quietly, in French.

'*Mais, madame* . . .' protested the faithful servant, but she was politely but firmly requested to return to the royal apartments and wait there. When she had gone, the surgeon effected the introductions before guiding his royal patient into a spotlessly clean examination room.

The Princess turned anxiously to look at Jacky. 'Are we alone?' she asked in English, the attractive accent betraying her French origins.

It was the surgeon who replied. 'I've sent the auxiliary medical staff off duty,' he assured her. 'Sister will help you to get ready for the examination.' He went into the outer room and Jacky was left alone with her patient.

It seemed strange to be helping a princess to undress! But after the outer garments had been removed and Jacky had produced a white gown she remembered only that this was a distressed patient who needed all the help and medical expertise she could give her.

'We're ready for you now, sir,' she told the surgeon, and took hold of her patient's hand in an automatic gesture. The Princess clung to it gratefully.

Dr Harvey bent over the patient and began his examination. Jacky couldn't help admiring the skill with which he calmed his patient while unobtrusively making a thorough abdominal and vaginal examination.

'I would say you're about fourteen weeks pregnant,' he said, pulling himself to his full height.

'I lost the last one at fourteen weeks,' the Princess announced in a deadpan voice. 'But I had felt ill for the whole of that pregnancy. And this time I feel marvellous.'

Dr Harvey smiled. 'I must say you seem to be in

excellent health. Sister will help you dress and then we can have a chat about treatment and so forth. There are absolutely no indications that we won't bring this pregnancy to full term.' He turned to Jacky and told her that the Princess had brought her medical notes with her from Reichenstein and recommended that she read them.

'I can manage to dress myself,' said the Princess gaily. 'Go and confer together. I'll come through when I'm ready.'

The doctor and Sister smiled at her new-found high spirits. 'I hope I'm not being too optimistic,' Dr Harvey told Jacky quietly when they were settled in his consulting room.

She looked at him carefully, surprised at his vulnerable tone. It hadn't occurred to her that the great man had feelings before. She had never even thought he was human during the long months since Chris's death. 'May I see the Princess's notes?' she asked gently.

The surgeon tossed a thin sheaf of papers on to his desk. 'She's kept these in her possession since the last miscarriage. As you can see, she underwent extensive tests to determine the cause and her doctors could find no abnormality such as congenital malformation, systemic disease or karotypic abnormality.'

'Would a Shirodkar suture help?' Jacky asked tentatively, remembering how the cervix was sometimes closed with a purse-string suture in cases of habitual abortion.

'I thought of that at first, but after examining her I can find no indication that this would help. There's no cervical incompetence.' The surgeon leaned back in his chair and frowned. 'It's a complete mystery why she miscarried, but I'm going to make damn sure it doesn't happen this time.'

Jacky was startled by the determination in his voice as he leaned across the desk to confront her.

'This is where you come in,' he told her earnestly. 'Women will always listen to another woman. It's almost as if they resent a man intruding on their female biological rights.'

She couldn't help laughing and for several seconds found it difficult to reply. 'I expect your theory has a grain of truth in it, sir, so what would you like me to do?' she asked gently.

He gave her a long slow smile and she held her breath as she watched the strong features relax. 'Together we must persuade her to rest, and then you must watch her like a hawk. She's a highly nervous individual, always on the go, hates doing nothing . . .'

His voice trailed away as the door opened and the Princess walked in. 'So what have you decided?' she asked briskly as she sank down into the chair which Dr Harvey had hastily held out for her.

'It's important that you rest,' the surgeon began.

'Rest, rest, rest!' the Princess repeated irritably. 'That's all my doctor could come up with last time!'

'And did you take his advice?' countered Dr Harvey swiftly.

The Princess gave a sly smile. 'Sometimes,' she replied, and gave a tinkling laugh.

'This time you *will* rest. And we must tell George . . .'

She put her hand on Dr Harvey's arm. 'But not yet, Carl,' she pleaded softly. 'I don't want him to know I'm pregnant when we go out to dinner this evening. The press will be watching, and George would be sure to give the game away. You know what he's like.'

'But do you have to go?' Jacky asked quickly. 'It would be much better if you stayed here and rested.'

Once more the Princess laughed. 'And can you imagine tomorrow's headlines if the press were told that I was indisposed?'

'I would prefer you to stay,' the surgeon told her, but she rose quickly and went towards the door.

'No, don't get up. I'll see myself out. Don't worry about tonight. I have total faith in the pair of you, and all I ask is that you stay close beside me. I'll ask George to arrange it.'

There was a faint aroma of French perfume as the Princess swept out through the door, a regal smile firmly on her lips. Jacky heard the outer doors close before she dared to raise her eyes to look at her boss.

He gave an exasperated sigh. 'Women!' was his first terse comment on the situation.

'Especially royal ones,' Jacky smiled.

'George is so soft with her. If she were my wife . . .' He broke off and gave an embarrassed grin.

'Yes?' she prompted. 'If she were your wife what would you do?'

'I'd keep her under control for a start,' he declared firmly.

'Do you think women should be kept under control—like animals, perhaps?' Jacky's tone was light, but there was a depth of intense feeling under it, and the surgeon sensed it.

'You're putting words into my mouth. I really don't think it's any concern of yours what I think.' He rose quickly and strode rapidly over to the door. 'Stay here and read the Princess's medical notes thoroughly so that you understand the case.' He turned with his hand on the door handle. 'There's no need to wear your uniform tonight. We shall be expected to mingle with the guests, but I want you to be near the Princess at all times.'

'Of course.' She bent her head over the case notes.

'Have a look at the Prince's notes while you're down here. He's a diabetic. I'll explain his treatment tomorrow . . . And don't be late this evening.'

Jacky looked up and smiled at the closing door. 'What an insufferable man!' she whispered to herself as she returned to her reading.

A cool evening breeze ruffled the case notes and she stood up to close the window. Glancing out, she saw an extensive rose garden that stretched almost to the shore of the lake. The early summer blooms filled the air with a strong heady perfume and she breathed it in before fixing the casement catch. It's such a romantic place! she thought as she sat down again on the expensive leather chair. There's an atmosphere of beauty and happiness everywhere. It's a house that's seen love and rich living; births, children, marriages, laughter . . . I'm not going to let Dr Carl Harvey spoil my time here!

It was almost dark before she finished perusing the medical papers. The time had been well spent, because she had learned all about the Prince's history of diabetes mellitus, the little Princess Helen's asthma and eczema and the seventy-year-old Dowager Duchess's angina.

'That's enough for tonight,' she told the empty room as she restored the case notes to the filing cabinet. At least I won't be totally ignorant when Dr Harvey briefs me tomorrow, was her main thought. It was important that she should gain his confidence so that, when the time was right, she could quiz him about why Chris had been chosen to test out an untried batch of insulin and why, after he had died no one would give her any information on the subject . . . certainly not the great director of the pharmaceutical company, Dr Carl Harvey, she thought bitterly as she went out through the swing doors and headed for her room.

Oh no, he had been far too busy to reply to her letter, she remembered. And the coroner's open verdict had done nothing to satisfy her curiosity. But she still had the brief note from Madeleine Cummings.

She smiled to herself as she went into her room. Yes, I still have that, she thought, and one day I'll confront him with it. I'll ask for an explanation. I'll tell him that I'm not satisfied with the way the case was handled.

She flung open her suitcase and started to throw things out on the bed in her distress. All the old agony rushed back. She hadn't known Chris Douglas long, but he had been fun to be with—at first. But then things started to go wrong between them. Chris had become more and more possessive, demanding more than she was prepared to give. It was obvious after only a few weeks that Chris was not her type, so she had tried to end their relationship, but Chris refused to believe that it was over between them. He told Jacky he couldn't bear life without her. But on the day that he died she had plucked up her courage and told him she didn't want to see him again. He had stormed out on her and said he hadn't time to argue.

'I have to go now, Jacky,' he had flung at her as he ran down the stairs from her room in the Nurses' Home. 'But I shan't give up. You don't mean it . . .'

'I do; I mean every word!' she had screamed down the stairs, but the slamming of the outer door had swallowed up her protests.

And that had been the last time she saw Chris. When the news filtered through that he had died from an overdose of insulin she had to admit that mingled with her natural sorrow, there had been a sense of relief that fate had solved the problem for her. But even as she thought this she was overwhelmed by a sense of guilt. She had never wanted such an awful thing to happen. Could it be that Chris had tried to commit suicide? she had wondered.

But all her efforts to find out what had really happened had drawn a blank. It was as if the pharmaceutical firm where Chris had offered himself as a paid guineapig in various clinical experiments had something to hide. At least, that was how Jacky interpreted their reticence and lack of co-operation. And in a way, it was a relief to transfer some of her own feelings of guilt about the way she had treated Chris on to the shoulders of the man in charge of the experiments. Yes, he was more guilty than she was, she figured. Dr Carl Harvey must own up to what had gone wrong. Only then would she be able to get on with her own life. Since Chris's death she had found it impossible to concentrate in the hospital where they had both worked. So when she had seen the post of Nursing

Sister to assist Dr Carl Harvey on an overseas
assignment advertised on the noticeboard, she had
offered herself before anyone else had a chance. It
seemed the great man was in a hurry to fill the post,
because she was seen only briefly by one of his
assistants, who was more than satisfied with her
references and qualifications.

It was a heaven-sent opportunity to get to the bottom
of things. One day soon I'll find out all the answers
from that supercilious Dr Carl Harvey, she vowed to
herself . . . but not yet . . .

CHAPTER TWO

THE PRESS were waiting for them when they boarded the cruise ship at the Atwater dock on the Detroit River. Cameras flashed as the royal entourage moved out from the fleet of limousines.

'There she is—there's the Princess,' cried one of the onlookers. 'Ooh, isn't she lovely!'

And Jacky, who was right behind the royal lady, had to admit that this was no understatement. Princess Karine was turned out to perfection in a cream silk creation which set off the royal diamonds to perfection. Jacky felt something of a Cinderella in her off-the-peg black full-length skirt and white frothy blouse, but nobody had warned her that she would have to attend an evening dress occasion on her first night here! I'll go and do some clothes shopping, she promised herself as she heard the whirr of a television camera close at hand.

'No need to worry about our patient,' whispered Dr Carl Harvey as they walked together over the red-carpeted gangplank. 'Doesn't she look wonderful?'

'Fabulous!' Jacky agreed, and raised her eyes briefly to survey the surgeon. He looks pretty fabulous himself, she admitted unwillingly as she noted the dark dress suit, the expensive white shirt and bow tie. If he had been anyone else she would have found him highly attractive.

He was holding out his hand to help her over the step into the cabin, and she smiled politely. He returned her smile, and again she couldn't help thinking how handsome he looked when his face relaxed into informality. Perhaps, just for tonight, I could try to forget who he is, she thought. It's a pity to hold a grudge in such superb surroundings.

She looked around her at the sumptuous fixtures and fittings. It was more like a luxury hotel than a ship, she decided; even to the chandeliers! Chandeliers on a ship! She wondered if they would jingle all night if you were in a storm at sea.

'Does this ship sail on the ocean?' she asked her escort.

The surgeon smiled. 'Not any more. It's used solely for entertaining—at a price, I might add! Our host is going to pick up a pretty hefty tab after all this.'

Jacky lowered her voice and asked who their host was. They were waiting to be presented to a tall grey-haired man and his elegant wife, and it occurred to Jacky that she had had no time to find out what the dinner was in aid of.

'He's the head of an international motor company,' Dr Harvey explained quietly. 'Prince George plans to open an assembly plant in Reichenstein using components made here in Detroit. This is going to help finance his new medical research centre. Our turn next . . .'

His hand was under her elbow as they were presented to their important host. The introduction lasted mere seconds before they moved on towards the royal table at the head of the dining cabin.

So Prince George is to have a new medical research centre in Reichenstein, Jacky thought as she allowed herself to be guided between the immaculate white tablecloths and sparkling glasses. I wonder who'll be the director of it. She smiled inwardly as they reached the royal table. The Prince had turned to snatch a few brief words with his old school chum and the two of them were grinning boyishly. It's a foregone conclusion, she told herself. Dr Carl Harvey will soon be exerting his doubtful authority over the Reichenstein institute, I expect.

The surgeon's hand was on the back of her chair as she took her allotted place at the table. A white-coated waiter leaned over from behind to fill her glass with champagne. She heard the tinkling laugh of the Princess and glanced at her briefly. She was rewarded with a confident smile before the Princess turned her attention once more to her host.

'I've never seen the Princess look so well,' Dr Harvey remarked as he took his place beside Jacky. Then he lowered his voice to say that he hoped Jacky would keep a watchful eye on her throughout the evening. 'I would prefer that she didn't dance,' he advised.

'I agree,' she said quietly, and then, after a brief pause, she asked, 'Tell me more about the new Reichenstein medical centre. Will you be involved, Dr Harvey?'

She raised innocent blue eyes upwards as she searched his face. He met her gaze, his brown eyes shining with excitement.

'Do you think you could call me Carl—especially off duty? We shall be working pretty closely together for the next few months and first names are so much easier. I'll call you Jacqueline.'

'Jacky,' she corrected hurriedly. 'Now, about the medical centre . . .'

'Oh yes; it's one of the most exciting projects I've worked on for a long time. Prince George has asked me to be the director, and I shall also be Professor of Surgery in the medical school. They're building a brand new hospital as part of the complex. It should be ready for use in October when the Prince returns to his country.'

'I believe you were involved in medical research in your previous position, weren't you, Carl?' Jacky slipped his name on the end of her seemingly innocent query, glad to be able to have a more friendly approach.

He looked surprised. 'Been checking up on me, have

you?'

She gave a hoarse laugh. 'Oh, come now, everyone must have heard of the great Dr Carl Harvey during his term of office at Chemico. Two illustrious years, wasn't it?'

There was a puzzled look in his eyes as he stared down at her. 'I'm flattered that you should have taken the trouble to research my background. I, on the other hand, know very little about you except that you were an exceptionally well qualified Sister at St Celine's in London and that they were sorry to lose you. Tell me, what made you resign and take this post?'

A waiter was serving her with fresh salmon and she pretended to focus all her attention on him while she tried to think of a suitable reply.

'I wanted to travel before it's too late,' she began tentatively.

'Too late?' Carl repeated with an amused grin. 'But you're a mere child; twenty-five, if I remember correctly?'

Jacky nodded. 'But I was becoming set in my ways. I needed a change. It's a mistake to carry on for too long at the hospital where you trained, don't you think?'

'Sometimes,' he agreed. 'It depends on the person. Certainly I've enjoyed travelling. I expect to settle in Reichenstein until I've got the project well under way and then I'll move on.' He paused and seemed to be searching for the right words. 'There could be a post for you out there if you wanted one. The Prince has asked me to recruit good medical staff while I'm in the USA. What do you think?'

'It's much too early to consider such an offer,' she said hurriedly. 'Let's get through this assignment first.'

Her heart was thumping rapidly. It was such a wonderful opportunity, but she couldn't possibly accept it. She took a sip of champagne and looked out across the spacious dining area towards where a band had

assembled and were beginning to play. As the first
strains of a haunting romantic melody drifted across she
heard Carl asking her if she would like to dance.

'Don't worry about Princess Karine,' he told her as
he saw her hesitation. He stood up as if to make up her
mind for her and she accepted his outstretched hand,
thinking that it would look strange if she refused.

The waiters were clearing the plates from the first
course and other couples drifted towards the dance
floor, but Jacky felt as if they were totally alone as Carl
took her in his arms. It was the strangest feeling as she
felt his strong hand in the small of her back. A shiver of
pleasure ran down her spine. My God, she thought
anxiously, is it so long since I was in a man's arms that I
have to react like this? I suppose I've been decidedly
frigid since Chris died—and let's face it, I've never met
anyone quite like Dr Carl Harvey before. Maybe it's the
danger and excitement of being in the arms of a man
you're planning to destroy. She raised her eyes to his
and saw that he had been studying her face with a
curious expression.

'Have we ever met before?' he asked, and an
enigmatic smile spread over his handsome face as he
waited for her reply.

'I don't think so. Otherwise I would have
remembered you. I've heard a great deal . . . about your
work,' she faltered.

His arm around her waist seemed to tighten its grip
and she found she was holding her breath.

'I visited St Celine's a couple of times when we were
looking for suitable medical students to help with our
research,' he told her nonchalantly.

Jacky's heart began to beat rapidly. This should be
her cue to ask if he remembered Chris Douglas. But she
couldn't risk a scene, here in the middle of the dance
floor, could she? No, this isn't the right time, she told
herself firmly. There'll be other more favourable

occasions, I'm sure. And it would be a pity to shatter this newly established intimacy so soon. In spite of herself she had to admit that she was enjoying the dance. She was also enjoying the admiring glances as the surgeon whirled her around the dance floor. It was a breathtaking experience in more ways than one, and she wanted it to go on and on . . .

When the music stopped, she found herself breathlessly holding on to her partner. Their eyes met and they both laughed spontaneously. Jacky admired the way Carl's usually immaculate black hair had a tousled effect; a deep wave had fallen across his wide brow, threatening to obscure the dark eyebrows and expressive brown eyes. She put a hand automatically to her own hair, which she had left loose for the evening instead of confining it to its workaday chignon on the top of her head. As she flicked one of the strands from her shoulder Carl put out a restraining hand and took some of the blonde hair in his hand.

'Leave it like that,' he said quietly. 'I like casual hair—especially when it's soft and shiny . . .'

She stared up at him and for a few seconds neither of them spoke. The other dancers were returning to their tables, but again Jacky experienced the distinct feeling that they were quite alone in the middle of the floor. It was the surgeon who broke the spell.

'But you'd better wear it up when you're in uniform,' he muttered abruptly as he steered her quickly back to her seat.

The main course was being served amid a flurry of silver salvers and tinkling cutlery. The waiters offered her a choice, and Jacky chose breast of veal stuffed with spinach served with a gratin of artichoke hearts and celery.

'I see the Prince is sticking to his diet,' Jacky remarked, and the surgeon seemed pleased by her interest.

'I'm glad you had time to study his case notes,' he replied with a smile. 'His condition has been stabilised and he's an excellent patient. I'm keeping him on 10,500 joules a day for his diet and he gives himself one injection of Lente insulin before breakfast. So far we've had no complications.'

When the main course had finished the guests began to dance again, and to her consternation, Jacky saw the princess rising to accompany her husband to the dance floor.

'Carl,' she muttered in consternation, 'what shall we do?' She had half risen in her seat, but sat down again when she felt his hand on her arm.

'There's nothing we can do now,' he whispered. 'We don't want to cause a fuss.'

'Perhaps you shouldn't have told the princess she was in excellent health,' Jacky told him. 'If you'd told her that her health was precarious she would have been more likely to take care.'

He frowned. 'But her health is not precarious,' he countered quickly. 'I always believe in telling the truth to my patients. It's a mistake to hide things from them.'

How can he be so two-faced! Jacky asked herself. I suppose he bends the truth to fit his own purposes. Her eyes followed the progress of the Prince and Princess as they circled the dance floor. Cameras clicked and the royal couple smiled and chatted happily, to the delight of the onlookers.

'At least it's a slow dance,' Carl remarked to her, and she nodded thankfully.

When the music stopped they breathed a sigh of relief.

'So far so good,' Jacky whispered.

Several of the male guests had come forward to enquire from the bodyguard if it would be possible to dance with the Princess.

Carl rose to his feet quietly and intervened. 'Princess Karine has had a heavy schedule today and her dancing partners must be restricted. I'm afraid that unless you've been informed of the possibility of a dance already then your request has been refused.'

'Who the hell's that?' Jacky heard one of the guests enquiring angrily, but she caught the thankful glance which the Princess gave to her doctor and decided that he would have made a good diplomat. She stared out of the wide portholes and saw the Detroit skyline lit up by the bright moonlight. Twinkling diamonds of light studded the tall buildings and bathed the scene with an aesthetic glow that was missing during the day.

'Would you like to go up on deck?' asked Carl as he saw her eyes straying to the striking panorama.

She hesitated. For some unknown reason she felt unwilling to be alone with him in the moonlight. But he was already on his feet. He asks a question and then answers it himself! she thought in exasperation, but her mood calmed at the touch of his fingers on her arm. He was so infuriatingly sure of himself, she thought as she allowed herself to be guided to the upper deck.

The ship was entering Lake St Clair as they leaned against the moonlit railings. Tiny pinpricks of light shone down from the cloudless sky, illuminating the dark surface of the water.

'Is that the house?' asked Jacky, pointing to a large brilliantly lit mansion sprawled out along the dim shoreline.

'Yes, that's it. No one would think the main occupants were out, judging by the number of lighted windows,' the surgeon remarked, relaxing his hold on the ship's rail to turn towards her.

She saw his profile outlined in the moonlight, strong, rugged, dependable. He's every inch the successful consultant, she found herself thinking. The sort of man that women patients swooned over—and nursing staff

too! Why couldn't he have been like I imagined him to
be? It would have been so much easier for me to do
what I have to do. She looked back across the twinkling
water towards the house.

'I suppose the place is full of servants,' she remarked
easily, remembering that the formidable Ms Cummings
would be back there working on her boss's
correspondence and fending off undesirable
applications for information. 'Who looks after the little
Princesses? Do they have a nanny?'

'Princess Karine prefers to be in charge of the
children herself now that they're out of the nursery
stage. Her maid Louise does all the chores, of course,
but the Princess likes to spend as much time with her
daughters as possible. And she takes them everywhere
with her,' Carl explained. 'Take this visit, for example;
the Princess refused to accompany the Prince unless the
girls could go along with her. In the end it was decided
to make a longer stay here and try to have an informal
family holiday in between the business negotiations,
which was why they leased that delightful house.' He
paused and stared out across the lake.

For several seconds there was a mutual silence
between them. Below on the lower deck Jacky could
hear the sounds of music and laughter and the clatter of
plates from the galley.

'Let's take a turn around the deck,' the surgeon
proposed amiably. 'The air's so good up here.'

She moved along as his arm guided her away from the
ship's rail. The ship was perfectly steady, but she felt
glad of his supporting arm lightly resting in the small of
her back. He's so gallant! she reflected unwillingly,
finding it difficult to concentrate on the spectacular
view. Another couple strolled past arm in arm in a
companionable middle-aged married sort of way. Jacky
felt a twinge of envy for the uncomplicated expression
on the woman's face. All passion spent, she deduced;

not quivering with apprehension at an impossible situation like me! Why don't I just ask him about Chris now?

She turned to look up at her companion. Yes, he looked very approachable now. 'Carl?' she began tentatively.

He stopped walking and stared down at her, intrigued by her curious tone of voice.

'There's something I'd like to ask you.' Her voice cracked on the last couple of words.

'Go on; I'm listening,' he assured her in a deep mellow voice.

'It's about your work at Chemico . . .'

He turned briskly and resumed his long strides. 'That's a very complicated subject and some of it's highly confidential. Would you mind awfully if we discussed it some other time? I think we should get back to our patient.'

He was already striding out in front of her; impossible to catch up with him! Yes, I do mind postponing the discussion, she longed to scream after him! But, on reflection, this was only what I'd expected, wasn't it? I can spot a guilty conscience by the way he's holding his head high so that I can't see his expression—even if I was able to keep up with his long legs . . .

The surgeon turned as he reached the stairs and smiled, seemingly unconcerned at her breathless state.

'Let's see if we can find some dessert,' he said boyishly. 'Would you like some strawberries?'

Jacky smiled politely. 'That would be delightful,' she said as she followed him back to their table. You've ducked out of the issue this time, she wanted to tell him, but next time I'll be more persistent, and you won't get away with it.

Carl snapped his fingers to attract the attention of one of the waiters.

'Bring some strawberries—and more champagne,' he requested, a broad smile spreading across his face. As the waiter topped up their glasses he turned to Jacky. 'Here's to a good working relationship,' he said smoothly.

She raised her glass to meet with his, but avoided his eyes. The wretched man was having a disturbing effect upon her, she admitted unwillingly. Not only was he avoiding her questions but he was making it difficult for her to remember the pain he had caused. She had only known him a few hours, but already she found herself wanting to please him, wanting to fall in with his plans . . .

'Is anything the matter, Jacky?' he asked gently as he put a long tapering finger under her chin, forcing her to raise her eyes.

The glint of a lone tear hovered in the corner of her eye and she hurriedly brushed a hand across it. 'I was remembering someone . . .' she began, desperately aware of his searching eyes. They held a mixture of sympathy and complexity.

'Someone close to you?' he asked softly.

She nodded, feeling encouraged by his tone. 'I didn't know him long . . .' Her voice tapered away as she thought, not now! It would be so awful to break up this feeling of warmth between them.

'One day you must tell me about him. I'm intrigued by your use of the past tense. Do I take it this relationship has ended?'

It was a perfectly normal assumption and Jacky had no desire to give any further details. Let him think what he liked for the moment! 'Oh yes, it's finished,' she told him. And yet again she experienced the awful feeling of guilt that had haunted her since Chris's death. She had wanted him to leave her alone; she had actually told him to go out of her life. It was as if fate had decided to take a hand . . . No, I mustn't think that, she told herself

firmly. It was the experiment that killed him, and it was
Carl who was in charge of that . . . If Chris had lived
longer we could have sorted out our differences and
remained friends. I didn't want him as a lover, but I
would have liked to see him again . . . if only to
apologise for some of the things I said in the heat of the
moment . . .

The Prince and Princess were returning from the
dance floor, she noticed, and the Princess seemed to be
leaning rather heavily on her husband's arm. Carl had
seen it too and was immediately on his feet. 'Come with
me,' he muttered under his breath.

As they reached Princess Karine's side she put out a
hand and took hold of the surgeon's jacket.

'Carl, thank goodness you're here!' she murmured.

He caught her in his arms as she fainted and was able
to scoop her up before anyone other than Jacky was
aware that there was anything untoward.

'It's much too hot in here,' the surgeon told her
dismayed husband. 'I'll take her out for some air . . .'
He had already reached one of the staircases and
retreated thankfully for a small band of curious
onlookers. Jacky was right behind him, with the Prince
hot on her heels.

'What's the matter with her?' the royal husband
clamoured when they were out of earshot.

'Too much excitement, delayed jet-lag; and it's too
damn hot in there.' The surgeon was playing for time.
'Ask them to turn up the air-conditioning, George,
before we get any more fainting cases. I'll take care of
Karine. You'd better go back to our host.'

The Prince hesitated, but Jacky convinced him it was
the best course of action. 'I'll fetch you if the Princess
needs you,' she finished, and Prince George returned
reluctantly to make a big fuss about the inadequate air-
conditioning.

Princess Karine opened her eyes as the doctor and

the Sister laid her on one of the beds in the ship's sick bay. 'Oh no!' she groaned. 'Did I faint?'

'I'm afraid so.' Carl shook his head. 'You were rather living it up tonight, Karine. But you're safe now. I've complained about the heat up there, so with any luck, no one will suspect anything. But we're going to take you home after I've examined you. Lock the door, Sister. We mustn't be disturbed.'

Minutes later, Carl pronounced that there were no complications but that the Princess must rest. He arranged for their speedy departure in a hurriedly summoned limousine. Messages were sent to the Prince saying that he was to remain at the party and not to worry about his wife. She was in excellent health.

It was after midnight before Jacky and Carl had settled their patient. The Princess was very tired and had readily agreed to going straight to bed, but not before Carl had persuaded her that she must tell Prince George about her condition. She promised to break the news to him in the morning.

'But you do think I'm going to be all right this time, don't you?' she asked fretfully.

'Only if you take care of yourself,' the surgeon replied a trifle harshly.

'Oh, I wlll!' the Princess assured him earnestly.

The surgeon and the Sister were reviewing the situation over a nightcap in the large drawing room.

'Do you think Princess Karine intends to be sensible?' Jacky asked her boss.

He shrugged. 'I hope so—but who can tell? She's a very stubborn lady. But I think tonight's little episode has frightened her. And the sooner George is in on the secret the better.' He paused reflectively and took a sip of his brandy.

'Do you think he will announce it to the press?' Jacky asked.

'I very much doubt it. He won't want to raise any

hopes until the baby is actually born—and he'll be praying for a son,' he added with a wry grin.

'What's so important about a son?'

'It's very complicated. There's a law of succession in Reichenstein which states that the throne passes to male heirs only. They've been having constitutional problems recently and the role of the monarch has been questioned. It would be a great relief if George had a son to succeed him.' Carl lowered his voice during the final sentence as the sound of the Prince arriving out in the hall came through to them. He put down his glass and stood up, his eyes nervously fixed on the ornate double doors that led out to the hall.

'How is she?' asked the Prince, bursting through the doors. 'I wanted to come sooner, but we were in the middle of negotiations.'

'She's fine.' The surgeon's tone was light, but he deliberately avoided looking at his royal friend.

'Level with me, Carl, for God's sake! You're holding something back. What is it? . . . She can't be pregnant . . .' The Prince stopped his anxious tirade as he looked from one to the other of them. '. . . can she?' he whispered after a few seconds.'

'You must ask her yourself, George—but not now; she's asleep and she needs all the rest she can get.' Carl sank back into his chair and took another sip of his brandy. He looked suddenly very tired, and Jacky found herself feeling very sorry for the invidious position that the Princess had placed him in.

The Prince's face creased into a deep smile. 'So she is pregnant!' he breathed happily. 'I wondered why . . .' He broke off and gave an uncharacteristic whoopee of joy. 'This calls for a celebration . . . We must have some champagne!'

He was striding towards the bell-pull by the fireplace, but Carl put out a restraining hand. 'We can't celebrate yet. Karine is only fourteen weeks; there's a long way to go. And George, please be surprised when she tells you tomorrow. Now go to bed—doctor's orders.'

The Prince smiled at his friend's peremptory tone. 'Yes, sir!' He uttered the words with a mock salute before moving towards the door. 'And Carl, thanks for everything,' was his final comment as he disappeared into the hall, the happy smile still on his face.

The surgeon breathed a sigh of relief when they were alone again. 'A difficult situation,' he reflected, 'when the patient asks for secrecy and her husband wants the truth.'

'I thought you handled the situation admirably,' Jacky put in quickly.

'Did you?' His eyebrows shot up quizzically and he seemed to be noticing her for the first time as a woman. 'You know, sometimes it's nice to have a little sympathy. People forget that doctors are only human. The emotional demands can be very demanding. But then you must have found this in your own nursing work, haven't you?'

She nodded. 'But it's very rewarding. I could never leave nursing.' She stood up and walked over to the window. It was getting late, but she felt unwilling to go up to her room. She was enjoying the company of a man who had caused her to suffer, and although the situation would be easier if she remained cold towards him, she found her resolve weakening. She looked out through the long French windows towards the lake. The lights of a late-night pleasure steamer twinkled on the dark water and the sound of distant music and laughter drifted across.

'It's a beautiful view.'

Carl's quiet tones interrupted her thoughts and she was surprised to find that he had joined her at the window. She could smell his distinctive aftershave as he looked out over her head.

She turned quickly and decisively. 'It's time I was

going to bed . . .' she began firmly, but she hadn't realised he was quite so close. Her eyes were on a level with his firm, aristocratic chin and he was smiling boyishly.

In a sudden swift movement he put his hands on her shoulders. 'Do I detect a feeling of fear?' he asked softly. 'You're a very unapproachable person, Jacky.'

'Am I? Perhaps I have reason to be,' she countered quietly.

'There's obviously something worrying you.' Nonchalantly he dropped a kiss on her forehead as if she were an obstreperous child. 'If there's anything I can do . . .' he began, but stopped mid-sentence and turned away.

Jacky watched him leaving the room with a murmured 'Goodnight' and then she was alone with her confused thoughts. Tomorrow, she told herself, I'll stop this procrastination and confront him. The sooner the mystery is cleared up the better!

But later, as she tossed in her luxurious bed, the doubts came rushing back. The royal surgeon was too good to be true! He was being deliberately nice to her to allay her fears. Maybe he knew who she was. She passed a hand over her moist brow and remembered the feel of his lips on her skin. It had moved her—oh yes, it had! she told herself unwillingly. Carl Harvey had a way of getting through to you. He was much too attractive, much too debonair and handsome! And I hate him, she thought unconvincingly as she drifted off into a troubled sleep.

CHAPTER THREE

BREAKFAST was taken in the dining room, a formal, elegant room whose walls were panelled with mahogany treated in a rich brownish tone and figured with roseleaf mottling. A white damask tablecloth covered the long table and provided the perfect background to the sparkling silver cutlery. Several places had been set, but only the surgeon and his secretary were seated when Jacky arrived. They were deep in conversation and barely acknowledged her entrance.

'If that's what you think then carry on,' Dr Harvey was telling his secretary. 'I trust your judgement . . .'

'But Carl, supposing he doesn't agree—what then?' Madeleine Cummings persisted.

'Then I'll step in and sort it out . . .' The doctor broke off and looked at Jacky. 'Help yourself to breakfast. It's buffet style—over there on the sideboard.'

'Thanks.' She noticed that he had lowered his voice to continue his discussion with his secretary. The two heads were close together when she returned with toast, orange juice and coffee.

'Is that all you're going to eat?' the doctor asked. 'You're as bad as Madeleine; she's permanently on a diet.'

'But I couldn't stay slim and beautiful if I over-indulged, now could I?' The secretary wrinkled her nose at her boss in a provocative manner.

He laughed. 'Women! I'll never understand them. I hope you won't faint mid-morning, Jacky, because we've got a lot of work to do.'

'Don't worry,' she told him smoothly, ignoring the piercing brown eyes. She was aware that they were both watching her as she spread marmalade on her toast. The surgeon had finished his breakfast and his secretary had merely taken a cup of black coffee. 'So what's the routine?' she asked after a few seconds of silence.

Madeleine Cummings gave a loud guffaw and then put a hand to her mouth as if to correct the unfeminine sound. 'There's no routine, my dear, not when you're working for Doctor Harvey. You must be prepared for anything. This isn't a general hospital, you know.'

'Thank you, Madeleine, I think Sister Diamond is perfectly well aware of the situation here. I'll give you a briefing in my office—as soon as you've finished your breakfast.' The surgeon rose from the table. 'And now if you ladies will excuse me . . .' He sauntered out of the room, seemingly unaware of the tension he was leaving behind.

'I shouldn't keep the doctor waiting if I were you,' began the secretary as soon as the door closed. She took a silver cigarette case from her crocodile skin bag and started to light up a tipped cigarette. 'You don't mind if I smoke, do you?' she added, almost as an afterthought.

Jacky put the last piece of toast in her mouth and chewed it slowly as she stared at the wisps of acrid smoke rising from her neighbour. When she had finished she stood up and pushed back her chair. If there was one thing that annoyed her it was the inconsiderate smokers who turned the question 'you don't mind if I smoke' into a statement! Still, if the poor woman had only had a cup of coffee to break her fast she would need to smoke to stave off the pangs of hunger, she told herself as she held back a retort.

'Carl hates me to smoke,' admitted Ms Cummings in a conspiratorial voice.

'I can imagine,' Jacky said drily as she made for the door. She was intrigued by the closeness of the doctor and his secretary. It's much more than a professional relationship, she deduced with a pang of resentment. As she walked down the long corridor with its massive china

vases standing like sentries on either side, she had to
conclude that she disliked the woman intensely. But she
was going to try hard to conceal her feelings Madeleine
Cummings obviously had influence over their boss, and
she didn't want to alienate him—yet!

Her boss was busily poring over some papers when she
went into his office. He looked up and smiled in an
encouragingly friendly way.

'Ready to start?' he enquired breezily, then without
waiting for an answer he leapt to his feet and came round
the desk. 'One of the maids is convinced she has
appendicitis, but I think it's only a menstruation pain.
Anyway, we'd better examine her.' He was ushering Jacky
out again and down the hall to the waiting area where the
unhappy girl was sitting hunched up on one of the chairs.
'Take her into the first cubicle and get her ready,' he
added.

The examination was a thorough one, and in spite of the
patient's moans and groans Carl was now convinced that it
was simply a case of dysmenorrhoea. He was satisfied that
there were no other complications apart from a severe case
of constipation.

'I'm going to give you a mild aperient,' he told the
patient. 'And you can spend the day resting in your room,
Julie.'

The girl's face lit up at this last prescription and most of
the symptoms seemed to disappear miraculously.

The doctor smiled. 'Yes, I thought that would cheer you
up. But I don't want you to be totally inactive. Take a
couple of hours's rest with a hot-water bottle and then get
up and move around the room. Come and see me again
next week.'

'Yes, Dr Harvey.' The maid sat up and Jacky began to
help her off the couch. 'Isn't he wonderful!' Julie said
when the surgeon had retreated. 'You're so lucky being
able to work for him. I think he should have been a film
star. He could easily be a doctor in one of those films on

TV; don't you think so, Sister?'

Jacky smiled. 'I think he prefers to be a real doctor, Julie. Do you like your work here?' she asked, changing the subject quickly.

'It's OK,' the girl conceded slowly. 'I'm only doing it to pay my way through college. I've taken six months off to earn some money and I'll be glad when it's time to go back to college. I work in a bar in the evenings when I'm in school and it's hard fitting in my studies, but it's more fun than this. It's so boring; dusting and polishing all day long . . .'

Jacky nodded sympathetically and went out to fetch the aperient. A day off will work wonders for her, she thought. Poor girl, stuck in a dead-end job!

'. . . I mean, I thought I was going to see life when I got this job with a real princess. Do you know, I've only ever seen her once!' The maid was still complaining as Jacky eventually showed her out.

There were several other servants waiting to be seen with minor complaints; a sprained wrist to be bandaged, a summer cold to be soothed, a maid who thought she might be pregnant but wasn't, and another two cases of constipation.

'I think I'll have to give a talk on nutrition,' Carl told Jacky with a wry grin as the last patient departed. 'It's not that the correct food isn't available, it's simply that some of the staff ignore the fruit and fibre in favour of the gooey cakes. And our first patient "Julie" is an ex-anorexic, so we'll need to keep an eye on her.'

'Really? Do you have any case notes on her?' Jacky asked quickly. 'Poor Julie; it's worse than I thought.'

Carl nodded. 'Over there in the filing cabinet. She's supposed to be cured, but these patients need following up for a long time. A year ago she weighed only four stone. It's all in the notes. Check it out when you've time, but not now,' he added quickly. 'The little Princesses are due any minute. You'd better have a look at their notes.'

There was barely time to read through the list of childhood ailments and ascertain that six-year-old Helen had eczema and asthma before the two little girls were ushered into the consulting room by the ever-faithful Louise.

'*Taisez-vous, mes enfants*,' the maid chided as she tried to stem their girlish chatter. Then with a great effort she switched to English to say, 'Good morning,' adding uncertainly, '*monsieur le docteur*.'

'Good morning, Louise,' the doctor replied. 'How is your mistress today?'

Louise looked puzzled, turning quickly to ask her charges. '*Qu'est-ce qu'il a dit?*'

Both little girls knew exactly what the doctor had said. Their English governess, back in Reichenstein, was aiming to make them fluent in English. They were happy to act as interpreters during the next few minutes, and Jacky complimented them on their English.

'Oh, we speak German too,' Charlotte stated easily with hardly a trace of an accent. 'We need all three languages in Reichenstein.'

'Perhaps Louise would like to go back to your mother,' suggested Carl, noting the incomprehension on the maid's face and also wanting to make sure that Princess Karine was well cared for. He had ascertained that she was in good health that morning, but he didn't want to take any chances. 'Sister can take you back to your room when we've finished.'

The message was relayed in French and the maid departed dutifully. Having glanced round the consulting room and subjected Jacky to a long scrutiny, Louise had decided that it was safe to leave her charges. And she too was anxious not to be away from her mistress for too long.

Charlotte's examination was merely routine. Carl wanted to check out for himself that the eight-year-old Princess was as healthy as her medical case notes suggested. As he removed his stethoscope at the end of the examination he gave a broad smile. 'Nothing to worry about, Charlotte. You're as fit as a fiddle.'

'What is a fiddle?' the little Princess asked, and Jacky was quick to explain the expression.

'I must tell my governess that I am as fit as a violin,' Charlotte said solemnly.

'Now it's your turn, Helen, or shall I call you Hélène?' Carl put in quickly as he hoisted the smaller Princess up on to the examination couch.

Her elder sister spoke for her. 'She's Helen in America and England, aren't you?'

The younger girl nodded obediently, and Jacky admired the long dark hair as the sun shone through the open window on to it. One girl for each parent, she noted; a dark-haired one like the mother and a sandy/auburn-haired one like the Prince. The elder Princess was the more self-assured—but maybe that's just the difference in age, she decided as she helped Carl to set the little girl at ease on the couch.

He was listening intently to her chest. When he straightened up he smiled encouragingly at his little patient, but Jacky could tell that he wasn't altogether satisfied.

'Have you had to use the inhaler I gave you?' he asked gently.

'She had to use it in the middle of last night,' put in Charlotte, eager to be helpful. 'Louise sat up with her for ages. She was making that funny noise—how do you say?—wheezing?'

Carl nodded thoughtfully. 'You should have called me. I'll tell Louise to ring me next time it happens.'

'I can tell her,' Charlotte said importantly. 'She doesn't understand English.'

The surgeon laughed and Jacky caught a glimpse of those devastating white teeth. He certainly has a way with girls, she thought—even little ones! They're obviously bowled over by him. She watched him pat the little heads of both Princesses as he told them that they would all instruct Louise and then maybe she would get the message.

'How's the skin?' he asked Helen, becoming serious again.

The small Princess pulled up her sleeve to reveal a large patch of eczematous lesions. 'This is the worst bit, doctor,' she told him quietly.

Carefully he checked all the areas of eczema before asking Jacky to apply a new ointment. She hesitated before asking,

'Has it been fully tested?'

He frowned. 'Of course it's been tested. Do you think I'd use it if it hadn't been?'

The little girl looked anxiously at the doctor and he hastily modified his tone. Once more the reassuring smile appeared as he repeated his request in an altra-polite voice.

'So, if you wouldn't mind applying the ointment, Sister . . .'

Jacky returned his smile, but underneath she was fuming. He's not going to ride rough-shod over me! she determined as she helped her patient off the couch. And I'm not going to fall for his suave ways and his debonair looks.

'The Duchess has requested that we visit her in her apartment,' her boss informed her amiably as she was finishing her skin application. 'We'll take the Princesses back on our way.'

He left instructions with the two auxiliary nurses as to his whereabouts for the next few hours and left the medical wing with a small girl clinging to each hand. Jacky walked behind, smiling to herself as she saw the way each girl vied with the other for the great man's attention.

They left the Princesses with Louise and proceeded down a long sombre corridor panelled in dark pine towards the apartment occupied by the Dowager Duchess, the Prince's mother.

'Don't allow yourself to be intimidated by the Duchess,'

Carl advised Jacky as they drew near to a large, heavily
carved door. 'She's a formidable character, but you must
remember she's only human. Concentrate on her medical
problems—that's what we're here for. You read her case
notes, didn't you?'

Jacky nodded thankfully.

The surgeon stopped outside the door and rang the bell.
The door opened and they were ushered inside. Jacky was
desperately trying to remember what she had read about
the seventy-year-old Duchess's angina as she looked round
at the luxurious interior. French walnut panelling framed a
large fireplace of grey sienna marble where, in spite of the
warm summer day, a log fire was burning. There was a
figure in the fireside chair hunched over a piece of
embroidery.

'*Monsieur le docteur est arrivé, madame,*' announced
the maid.

'*Quoi*?' The Duchess looked from her tapestry and a
slow smile spread over her old, wrinkled face. 'Oh, it's
you, Carl,' she said in a relieved voice. 'I thought I had
visitors; can't stand visitors in the morning. I never look
my best until after dark. Candlelight has been my greatest
ally since I turned forty. 'She screwed up her eyes and
stared at Jacky. 'Who's this?'

'May I introduce Sister Jacky Diamond . . . Her Royal
Highness the Duchess . . .'

'Oh, never mind all that, Carl; what's she doing here?'
interrupted the Duchess irritably.

'Sister Diamond is helping me to run the medical
facilities here,' the surgeon explained patiently.

'Come nearer, Sister . . . ah, now I can see you're
wearing one of those pretty uniforms . . . mm, very nice,'
the old lady commented, removing the embroidery from
her lap to a nearby table. 'Well, what do you both want?'

'You sent for me, ma'am,' replied Carl gently.

'I did?' The Duchess looked puzzled. Her diminutive
features creased into a frown and she shrank back in her

chair like a tiny bird. 'Oh, now I remember; I had another
of my pains in the night—was it last night, Gisèle?' She
addressed her maid in English but repeated the question in
French when she saw the look of incomprehension.

Jacky gathered that the Duchess had been awake for
most of the night suffering from severe chest pains, but
they had responded to a capsule of amyl nitrate
administered by Gisèle.

Carl insisted on an immediate examination in the
Duchess's bedroom. When he was satisfied that the danger
had passed he left instructions that he was to be called at
the first sign of another attack.

Day or night—it doesn't matter when; just call me,'
were his final words as they took their leave. The Duchess
had agreed to spend the day in bed as a precaution, and
they left her surrounded by all the trappings of her
luxurious life-style yet looking like a child who has been
kept inside for misbehaving. The gnarled old hands lay
over the silken coverlet in an attitude of despondency and
there was a sulky set to the royal mouth as the old lady
watched her medical advisers depart.

'I expect she'll get up as soon as she thinks we're out of
the way,' Carl told Jacky as they walked down the
corridor away from the Duchess's apartment. 'Then she'll
go back to bed just before I'm due to arrive this evening.
Sometimes I think it's a mistake being the doctor of
someone you've known for a long time. She doesn't take
me seriously . . . still thinks I'm a schoolboy.' He grinned
and shook his head amiably.

'How long have you known the Duchess?' Jacky asked.

'Since George first took me over to Reichenstein for the
summer holidays. I was jolly scared of her, I can tell you!
Well, I suppose I was only about seven at the time . . .' His
voice petered away and a faraway look came in his eyes.

'You were at boarding school when you were seven,
were you?'

Carl nodded. 'Yes, my parents travelled a great deal and

it was the easiest way of solving the problem . . . the problem of looking after me,' he clarified quickly.

They had reached the swing doors of the medical wing and Jacky went through as he held one of them open. In her mind's eye she could see the little Carl as a child. He would have been thin—even spindly perhaps—because he was lean as an athlete now at the advanced age of—whatever it was. She eyed him thoughtfully. Yes, he was probably thirty-five, she decided, as her careful scrutiny revealed a couple of grey hairs lurking amid the dramatic black . . .

'What are you thinking?'

His question interrupted her reverie and she focused on his brown eyes, which held a puzzled look.

'I was thinking that seven is very young for a boy to be away from his parents. Didn't you have any other brothers or sisters?'

He smiled. 'No; I was an only child.' His voice changed abruptly as one of the auxiliary nurses appeared to ask him about treatment for one of the gardeners who had cut himself while sawing up logs.

The professional relationship was resumed as Jacky cleansed the wound and Carl put a couple of sutures in, followed by an anti-tetanus injection.

'I have to go over to the Detroit Medical Center this afternoon,' he told her at the end of the morning. 'I'm recruiting for Prince George's new medical project in Reichenstein. I'd like you to hold the fort here until I get back. You can give me a buzz at this number if there's something you can't handle. Do you think you can cope?'

Jacky took the card with the phone number from her boss. 'Of course I can cope,' she told him easily.

'I thought we could go out to dinner this evening,' he stated quietly.

She flashed him an enquiring look, surprised that he should assume she would want to go out to dinner with him. Again she reflected that he was so sure of himself!

'There are a number of things we must discuss, and it's always easier over the dinner table,' he continued as if sensing her reluctance.

'I have no other plans for this evening,' she told him carefully.

'I'll book a table at Mario's.' He closed his report book decisively and stood up. 'Until this evening . . .'

Jacky watched him stride over to the door, heard his footsteps in the outer hall and listened for the swing of the doors before she moved.

'Shall I clear up now, Sister?' asked the young American auxiliary nurse.

'Yes, please,' Jacky replied absently. She was still thinking about the young boy of seven who had spent his summer holidays with the royal family of Reichenstein. What an experience for one so young! but she was glad that she had not had to leave her parents at such a tender age. There was something very comforting about having a normal family background, she decided as she went out into the examination area to help her nurse. As she cleared away the dressings and reset the trays her mind turned to thoughts of home life as she knew it. Her parents were supportive but never pushy with their ideas. She knew that she was always welcome at home, but she never felt that she had to do the dutiful visits. Her mother, a teacher, had pursued her career while bringing up her family, but neither Jacky nor her elder sister ever felt neglected. Their mother had always found time for them even after a long day in school and an evening spent marking books.

And Jacky had always been able to take her friends home and had never been criticised even when she knew that her parents disapproved of the occasional acquaintance. Chris had been just such a one, Jacky remembered. She had known as soon as they sat down to supper in her mother's kitchen that her parents were finding it a strain to be polite to their guest.

Jacky plunged a kidney dish into the steriliser, and as

the haze of steam cleared she remembered the awful silence that had fallen over the kitchen table after Chris had told a rather risqué joke. It was not that her parents were prudish, but Jacky herself had thought the joke in very bad taste, and she could see that Chris was in one of his hyperactive moods. He hadn't wanted to spend the evening with Jacky's parents, but she had promised to go and see them. They were expecting her, and Chris had gone along rather than spend the evening alone.

Her mother had thought it was to be a quiet family evening and had prepared only a small casserole for the three of them. Her father had come in from the office, having battled with the commuter train at the end of a long hard day, and was hoping to escape from the table to his favourite chair and a good book. But, Jacky remembered with a rueful smile, the arrival of an unexpected guest had been accepted with fortitude. Her mother had smiled and cleared away her exercise books from the table and her father had made interesting conversation—until Chris had spoiled the atmosphere with his crude joke. Even then, it had only been obvious to Jacky that something was wrong. Chris had been totally oblivious of his faux pas.

Yes, she had a lot to be thankful for in coming from a warm secure background. And her parents' reaction to her announcement that she was going to nurse in the States had been typical of them. They thought it was a good opportunity for her; they would miss her, but they wouldn't stand in her way. And there would be a warm welcome when she next went home again, just as there had always been. She had been careful not to mention her continued involvement with Chris Douglas. She knew that her parents considered that episode in her life was finished.

If only it could be! Jacky tossed a clean sheet on to an examination couch and tucked in the corners with an over-vigorous precision as she thought how wonderful it would be if only she could let go of this obsession with Chris. All my life I seem to have attracted lame ducks! she thought.

It's my own fault, I suppose. I'm too soft-hearted. I can't help taking other people's worries on to my own back. She remembered the times that Chris had told her about never knowing who his real parents were when he was a child. He had been adopted when he was a baby and he had never felt close to his adoptive parents. When he was eleven they were killed in a car crash, so he was put in a foster-home, which he hated.

'Poor Chris!' she sighed out loud.

'Is something the matter, Sister?' The young American nurse looked into the cubicle.

'Everything's OK,' Jacky said hurriedly. 'It's time you were off duty. Run along; I'll finish up here.' She smiled at the girl's sympathetic face. Funny how we nurses tend to be endowed with sympathy, she thought as the girl went out through the swing doors. It's a necessary part of our character if we're to make good nurses, but it can also be something of a curse if you get caught up with a character like Chris Douglas!

She put the finishing touches to the couch and went out into the corridor, still thinking about Chris's problems. She remembered how he had told her that he had searched out his real mother during his first term at medical school. He had thought she would be proud of the fact that her son was going to be a doctor, but instead she had asked him to keep his identity quiet. Apparently, she was unmarried and ashamed of the fact that she had borne an illegitimate child.

As she ran up the stairs to her room, Jacky made a determined effort to put him out of her thoughts for a while.

In the middle of the afternoon, Jacky was summoned to Princess Karine's sitting room.

'It's nothing important, Sister,' the Princess began as she noticed the concerned look on Jacky's face. 'I just wanted to have a chat with you. Do you take tea?'

Jacky gave a relieved smile. 'Yes, I do, Your Highness. . .'

'Oh, let's dispense with the formalities, please. If you're working with Carl I would prefer you to call me Karine as he does—in private, of course.' She gave a tinkling laugh as she poured tea from a delicate china pot. 'Cream or lemon?'

'Lemon, Your . . . lemon, please.'

They both laughed now and the ice was broken. Jacky knew that she would be able to address the Princess by her first name soon—but not yet! She had to get used to the idea first. She noticed that the servants had been dismissed from the room. Even the watchful Louise was nowhere to be seen.

'I want to talk to you woman to woman,' began the Princess quietly. 'This is the first time we have all been away from Reichenstein together. It was meant to be a family holiday—apart from the fact that George has some business negotiations to attend to.' She gave a delightful grin and shrugged her narrow shoulders. '*C'est normal* . . . we're used to mixing business with pleasure, but now . . .' Her voice trailed away and she paused as if searching for the right words. '. . . Now that I'm pregnant I'm going to have to take things easy, and I don't want my daughters to suffer because of this. I had planned to do so many things with them—visit Niagara Falls, go whale-watching at Cape Cod. They've been so looking forward to this summer and now, in a way, I feel I've spoiled it for them.'

Jacky drew a deep breath. She was going to have to tread very carefully. Whatever she said was going to have a profound effect on her patient. She must forget that this was a royal princess and remember only that Karine was a mother torn between loyalties, as mothers always have been, since the beginning of time . . .

She stared round at the ornate, luxurious room. The alabaster figures on the ceiling looked back at her in doleful silence, offering no help whatsoever. 'Carl and I don't intend to wrap you in cotton wool until your baby is born,' Jacky began carefully, 'but at the same time, in view of your medical history, you're going to have to make your unborn baby your priority. The girls will have to take second place until after the birth. I think the easiest way of getting round this is to enlist their help.'

The Princess looked puzzled. 'What do you mean?'

'One day they too will be women, and this is an excellent time to start teaching them what it's all about. Explain that you're going to give them a baby brother or sister. Say that usually this is a normal affair, but because you've had some abnormal medical problems, you have to be extra careful with your health. That's not too difficult for them.' Jacky watched her patient carefully as she digested the information.

'Will you come here when I tell them?' Princess Karine asked uneasily.

'Of course I will; they'll be over the moon about the baby. And don't worry about the outings when you can't go with them. We'll sort something out . . .'

The Princess interrupted her enthusiastically. 'Of course! You and Carl could stand in for me. They adore Carl—who wouldn't!—and if you were there to help him—well, it would be a perfect situation. Charlotte is longing to see Niagara Falls, and I promised Helen she could watch the whales off the coast of Cape Cod.'

'I didn't exactly mean that . . .' Jacky tried to put in, but her disquiet passed unnoticed.

'George is always too busy to take the girls out, and anyway, someone usually recognises him, but Charlotte and Helen have been deliberately kept out of the limelight. If they were with you and Carl and you all dressed in casual clothes . . .'

The Princess continued her praise of the plan that had evolved, and Jacky hadn't the heart to interrupt her. Whatever will Carl say? she wondered uneasily as she placed her thin china cup on the tea tray. I have no idea how he'll react. I know so little about him . . .

'More tea, Jacky?' The Princess turned her attention away from her own problems.

'No, thanks I must return to the medical wing, Karine.' There! I've said it, she congratulated herself, and it didn't seem difficult.

'You've been such a help,' the Princess told her as she accompanied her to the door.

Later that afternoon, as Jacky was closing up the medical wing, she began to feel apprehensive about having dinner alone with her boss. Not only was she going to confront him about his rôle as director of the pharmaceutical firm responsible for Chris's death, but also she would have to admit that she had allowed herself to fall in with the Princess's plans for the summer! She didn't know which admission was going to be the more difficult.

CHAPTER FOUR

MARIO'S restaurant was located in downtown Detroit. Prince George had insisted that Carl and Jacky be taken there in a royal limousine by one of the chauffeurs.

'Do you want me to wait, sir?' the young man asked, standing smartly to attention on the kerbside. His deferential manner and military-style uniform were attracting curious glances from the evening strollers, some of whom were unashamedly advancing closer to get a better look at the obviously important couple.

'No, thanks,' Carl told the chauffeur hurriedly. 'We'll get a cab when we come back.' he tucked his hand under Jacky's arm, reflecting that he hadn't wanted the royal limousine in the first place. It was much better to travel around incognito.

As Jacky walked through the open door of the restaurant she heard one of the onlookers saying,

'Isn't that the foreign princess . . . what's her name?' The man had stepped forward enquiringly.

'That's not Princess Karine,' his wife told him impatiently. 'The Princess is dark-haired and this one's a blonde. No, I don't know . . .'

Jacky smiled to herself and pulled herself to her full five feet six. It isn't every day you're mistaken for a princess, she reflected. So it was worth the extra time she had spent getting ready, and she was glad she'd worn her new cream suit. It had been her one extravagance before she left England. And now, teamed with the dusty pink silk blouse she'd picked up in a Harrods' sale, she was feeling good. The high-heeled black patent sandals matched her bag—another find in the sales!—and elevated her so that her eyes were on a level with the middle of the surgeon's head instead of somewhere around his chin.

'Come this way, sir. Your table is ready . . .'

'We'll have to drink at the bar first,' Carl told the waiter in a leisurely voice.

Jacky enjoyed the admiring glances as Carl steered her towards the bar. She perched on a high stool as her boss ordered the drinks and wondered if she would like the cocktail he had recommended. The surgeon was looking decidedly pleased with himself, she acknowledged, and devastatingly handsome. There was something about the way his mouth seemed to curve automatically into a smile as if he didn't have a care in the world.

'Two Manhattans,' the barman announced, placing the clinking glasses on the bar.

'Cheers!' The surgeon had raised his glass and Jacky followed suit.

'Mm, that's nice,' she pronounced after a tentative sip. 'What's in it?'

'Cinzano and Canadian Club,' he informed her easily while an amused grin spread over his face. 'Is this your first visit to the States?'

She nodded. 'I've always wanted to see America . . .'

'What's the matter?' he asked as he saw her hesitate.

Jacky took a deep breath as she thought how it would be better to take the bull by the horns and tell her boss about Karine's suggestion. 'Would you mind if we did some sightseeing together? You see, Princess Karine suggested we could stand in for her when she can't accompany the little Princesses. I mean, now that she's pregnant she can't be expected to rush around with her daughters, and they were so looking forward to their holiday. It would be a shame to disappoint them, wouldn't it?'

She took a gulp of her Manhattan and almost choked as she reflected that she was not making much sense. But the wretched man looks so smooth and suave, she told herself by way of excuse. It's no wonder he makes me feel nervous.

Carl had put his drink down and turned to face her.
'Let's get this straight,' he said in a cool, distant voice.
'Are you saying that the Princess has put forward an idea,
or have you agreed—in my absence?'

'It was difficult not to agree. I mean, she just sort of
assumed,' Jacky rushed on breathlessly. 'And I thought
that in the interest of our patient . . .'

'Don't give me that!' His raised voice brought the
barman scurrying across to ask if everything was all right.
Carl gave a tightlipped smile and waved him away. Then,
lowering his voice, he confronted Jacky again. 'Let me
remind you that I make the decisions around here . . . In
the interests of the patient indeed! . . . Let's go and dine.'

Jacky followed the irate figure through to the candlelit
dining room. Miserably she allowed the waiter to pull out
her chair in a cosy recessed alcove. Her mind barely took
in the rich surroundings, the panelled walls enlivened by
large oil paintings of Venice and the soft, pastel hues of the
thick carpet.

'Don't look so sad.'

The feel of Carl's hand on hers as he leaned across the
table made her look up, startled at this sudden change of
mood. 'You must realise that I dislike insubordination. If
we're to have a good working relationship then you must
always consult me. Is that clear?'

She nodded as she met his gaze. She couldn't believe
how gentle his tone could be now after the harsh
indictment. Her fingers lay limp inside his grasp and she
hadn't the slightest desire to remove them. There was
something decidedly pleasant about the feel of her arm on
the white tablecloth. And his face looked so romantic by
the light of the candles . . .

'Would you care to order now, sir?'

'Not yet,' Carl told the waiter without taking his deep
brown eyes from Jacky's face. He wanted to get to the
bottom of this. 'What have you agreed?' he asked gently.

She felt a faint squeeze of his hand as she stared back at him. He's trying the bedside manner on me now, she thought resignedly. I'm nothing more than a tiresome woman to him.

'I've agreed to help the Princess by taking the children sightseeing. In view of her delicate condition . . .' she began, but he removed his hand and sat back in his chair with an amused laugh.

'So we're back to the medical necessity of all this are we? Well, you certainly know how to get round a fellow! Just where are we supposed to take the royal darlings?'

His face was still relaxed and smiling, Jacky noticed with relief as she continued her explanation. 'Oh, the usual places out here.' She shrugged her shoulders. 'You know, Niagara Falls . . .'

'But that's miles away!'

'And Cape Cod.' Might as well be hanged for a sheep as for a lamb, she figured as she hurried on nervously.

'Cape Cod?' Carl repeated almost in disbelief. 'I haven't time to go down to Cape Cod. There's so much to be done here in Detroit before we go back to Reichenstein . . .'

'Not even for two little princesses whose mum is having a baby?' Jacky put in quietly.

For a second she thought he was going to be angry with her again. She held her breath as she watched him digest her latest attempt at pacification. Oh well, I've put my foot in it well and truly, so I've nothing to lose, she figured. As the smile on his face broadened she breathed an audible sigh of relief.

'I think you could sell fridges to the Eskimos,' he concluded. 'Niagara Falls I can understand, but why Cape Cod?'

'To watch the whales,' Jacky murmured, keeping her eyes studiously on the rich nap of the tablecloth.

'But of course. I should have know . . . We're ready to order now,' he told the hovering waiter, who hurried forward.

She couldn't tell how he felt about the whale-watching proposal, but his sarcastic tone indicated that he had no wish to pursue the subject further, and that was fine by her! She wanted to restore some of their former feeling of cordiality and make the most of her evening out.

'The cannelloni here is superb—you do like Italian food, don't you, Jacky?'

She nodded, thinking that it was a bit late to ask now! 'I love it.'

'Cannelloni to start, followed by *faraona* and some *insalata verde*. And we'll have a bottle of *vino rosso*.' Carl was studying the wine list carefully. 'Let me see . . . this one will go rather well.'

'What's *faraona*?' asked Jacky when the waiter had departed.

'Guinea-fowl,' he told her, adding, 'You *must* like guinea-fowl.'

'Must I?' She raised wide eyes to his, wanting to challenge his assumption that he was always right, but decided not to break the atmosphere of truce between them. 'I do, as a matter of face,' she conceded, but decided not to tell her high-handed boss that she had only tasted it once at a dinner-party. Guinea-fowl didn't appear on the menu in the hospital canteen, she almost told him.

The delicious food and wine helped to ease the tension. In fact Jacky felt positively enamoured of her companion by the time she had polished off a plate of profiteroles at the end of the meal. The waiter brought strong black coffee in tiny cups and she sat back in her chair, enveloped in a warm glow of contentment.

'You look so much younger when you're relaxed,' Carl said quietly. 'And prettier,' he added as his eyes searched her face appraisingly.

'Thank you, kind sir,' she quipped easily, feeling furious at the blush which had suddenly suffused her face. If only he would stop staring at her! 'Tell me about your work here in Detroit . . . I mean, you said you had such a lot to do before you went back to Reichenstein with Prince George.'

'Mainly recruitment for the new medical project. We've got to get the right kind of staff. I'm still looking for someone to take charge of the pharmaceutical research so that I can concentrate on surgery again,' he told her wistfully.

'Do you miss the operating theatre?' she asked gently.

'Oh, very much,' was his passionate reply. 'It used to be my whole life . . .'

'So what made you change to pharmaceutical research?' She was keeping her tone deliberately light.

'I needed the money.' Carl stopped abruptly as if regretting the admission. 'Would you like some more coffee?'

Jacky shook her head. 'No, thanks . . . You mean, you couldn't manage on the salary of a consultant surgeon?' she queried in disbelief.

'Not at the time,' he replied in a measured tone.

'But what made you leave Chemico after only two years?' She was trying to conceal her excitement at being able to question the great man in such intimate surroundings. She had never dreamed she would get such an opportunity.

'This is turning into an interrogation,' he told her abruptly. 'Why are you so interested in my affairs?'

'Because I was a friend of Chris Douglas.' There, she'd confessed! She hoped she hadn't mistimed it. What a pity it would be if he refused to explain anything.

For an instant Carl stared at her perplexed, then something seemed to jog his memory. 'You were a friend of Chris Douglas?' he repeated. 'So that's why you've been hounding me!'

'I'm only after the truth,' she flung at him.

'Isn't everyone?' was his weary reply. 'I'm sick of the whole unfortunate incident.'

'But what happened? Why did he have to die? Why did you let him be the guinea-pig for something so dangerous as an untried batch of insulin?'

'Steady on!' he ordered brusquely. 'You know nothing of the circumstances . . .'

'Of course I know nothing, because you've refused to discuss it. You were in charge and therefore you're responsible for what happened. He was a penniless medical student who needed the money, just as you needed money when you had to leave surgery . . .'

'There's a phone call for you, sir.' The waiter broke through her tirade to plug a phone in by their table.

As Carl picked up the instrument he looked relieved to be off the hook. Jacky breathed evenly as she bided her time. He wasn't going to get away so easily, she was thinking.

'Yes, of course I'll come at once,' he said quickly.

Her heart sank as she realised that their discussion would have to end and also there must be some sort of emergency back at the royal household.

'Get a cab,' Carl ordered the waiter brusquely. 'And bring the check—*subito*! It's the Prince,' he told Jacky. 'Sounds as if he's in a diabetic coma. I can't think what can have gone wrong . . .'

The cab raced through the secluded Grosse Pointe Avenue. Jacky could see the lights of the royal mansion as they drew near to the lake. I hope we're in time, she prayed silently.

Louise and the auxiliary night nurse were standing on the steps waiting for them.

'Oh, doctor, thank goodness you're here!' exclaimed the uniform-clad girl. 'The Prince came down to the medical wing to say he was feeling ill and then he passed out on me. I didn't know . . .'

But Carl was already going into the house, a grim expression on his face as he headed for the medical wing.

Jacky followed her boss quickly. Through the swing doors she found the Princess pacing the floor in agitation. 'He's in here,' she blurted out in relief.

The unconscious figure of the Prince lay on one of the examination couches while the day nurse, hastily roused from her bed, was bending over him taking his pulse.

'What happened, nurse?' Carl snapped.

'He was sweating profusely, sir, when he came down. And he complained of feeling dizzy. I told him to lie down. That was when I phoned you, sir. His pulse is very rapid,' the young nurse reported anxiously.

'He missed dinner this evening,' the Princess put in quietly. 'There were some important papers he wanted . . .'

'But you should have made him eat dinner.' Carl rounded on Princess Karine as if she were a naughty schoolgirl. 'You know my instructions.' He suddenly became aware of the enquiring glances made by the rest of the staff and modified his tone. 'Perhaps Your Highness would like to return to your room. I will keep you informed of the Prince's progress. Louise, take care of your mistress.'

'*Qui, monsieur le docteur.*' For once, the French maid had understood.

'Sister, I'm going to inject 0.5 ml of 1:1000 adrenaline solution stat. Get it for me...thanks...hold his arm. . .'

Jacky swabbed the Prince's arm, thinking how damp and clammy the skin felt. It was a typical case of hypoglycaemic coma brought on because the patient had not taken sufficient carbohydrate to counteract the effect of his insulin dose.

'We'll set up an intravenous infusion of glucose, Carl told her briskly. 'That should bring him out of the coma.'

They worked together side by side until they were rewarded by a flickering of the royal eyelids.

'What on earth? . . . Where am I?' The Prince stared around him in confusion.

Who's been a naughty boy, then?' said Carl in a

bantering tone.

Jacky smiled to herself at the surgeon's words. There was no royal protocol between the old school friends. The staff had long since retired to bed and only she and Carl were left to witness the Prince's discomfort.

'Oh God, I'm sorry,' the Prince mumbled. 'Can I have a drink of water? I'm so thirsty. I remember coming down here. I'd forgotten you'd gone out. And that dear little nurse helped me on to the couch. The room was swimming round . . . ooh, my head!'

'And all because you missed your supper. Don't you remember that time at school? You promised Matron you'd stick to your diet. Anyway, I'm glad you've pulled through, old man.'

Jacky noticed the husky relief in the surgeon's voice as he began to dismantle the IV. It was only then that she began to understand the depth of his anxiety. She had been able to stand back and view the patient professionally, but Carl had been resuscitating an old friend.

'Can I go back to my room?' the Prince asked tentatively.

'Not yet. You'd better stay here where I can keep an eye on you. And in the morning we'll have to run a series of tests so that we can get the diabetes under control again. Would you prepare a bed, Sister?'

The doctor's eyes barely focused upon her as he issued the order. It's a cool professional relationship, Jacky thought as she hurried away to prepare a bed. He's probably forgotten he took me out to dinner this evening. I'm just another link in the chain of minions who pander to his every whim . . . But he did a good job on the Prince tonight, she admitted grudgingly. He's a good doctor. She turned back the top sheet and plumped up the pillow.

'Ready?' Carl was standing in the doorway supporting his patient. She moved to help him and together they eased the Prince in between the sheets.

'I'll stay with him,' Carl told her as he sank down into

an armchair near the bedside. 'You run along—and Jacky, thank you for your help.' His mouth curved into a weary smile. She noticed that his black hair was damp with sweat from the exertions of the night.

'You look tired,' she volunteered sympathetically. 'Would you like me to relieve you later on—say, in a couple of hours?'

He shook his head. 'I'll be all right. Go to bed.'

That last picture of the exhausted surgeon stayed with Jacky as she fell asleep. She could remember the line of his muscular jaw, the tousled mop of hair hanging over his forehead and the sensitive hands lying still on the arm of the chair. It was impossible to dislike the man—even though he had avoided her questions and given incomplete answers to those she had managed to put to him. What was she to make of him? she asked herself, and unwillingly admitted that she wished Carl had not been involved in Chris's death; because in spite of everything she found him desperately attractive and knew that she would have to work very hard at not falling in love with him . . .

The cold light of day brought Jacky to her senses and the brusque orders issued by her boss put her feelings back into perspective. She hoped he would keep up his cool professional manner; it made it so much easier for her to think rationally. The tests on the Prince kept them occupied during the morning, in between coping with the staff medical problems. Madeleine Cummings spent the morning in the outer office dealing with Carl's correspondence. She flitted out occasionally to ask him questions in a soft silky voice which betrayed how besotted she was with her boss. Jacky almost collided with her at one point as she carried a heavy tray from the Prince's room.

'My, we are in a hurry this morning!' Madeleine said as she glanced down at her skirt to see that nothing had been spilled over it.

'It's rather congested in here today,' Jacky returned in a cool voice as she prepared to pass.

'Do I detect a slight hangover? Too much of the *vino rosso* at Mario's?' the secretary enquired with a saccharine smile. 'The last time Carl took me there . . .'

'Haven't you ladies anything better to do than chat in the corridor?' The surgeon towered above them as he attempted to go inside the Prince's room. 'When you've unloaded that tray I need you in here, Sister . . . oh, and Madeleine, get that report typed up before lunch.'

'Of course,' smarmed the secretary, but Jacky turned on her heel and made off in the other direction as quickly as she could. As she threw the disposable syringe and needle away she reflected that Madeleine had done her a service by telling her that she was not the only one to be taken out for a candlelit dinner.

When she returned to the Prince's room, Jacky found that the Princess had arrived. Carl was trying to reassure her that all would be well once the diabetes had been put under control again.

'And then it will be up to you to see that George behaves himself,' he said with a wry grin. 'How are you feeling this morning?'

'Never felt better,' the Princess told them with a happy smile. 'Do you think I'm going to make it this time?'

'I don't see why not,' Carl replied in a cautious voice.

'If you can give me a son and heir I shall be the happiest man in the world,' put in the Prince earnestly.

'Hey, who said anything about a son?' the surgeon asked hastily, anxious that the Princess should be relieved of too many pressures. 'We're hoping for a healthy baby, that's all.'

'I know, but I'm praying for a son,' the Prince replied in a fervent tone. 'Do you think you could arrange for Karine to have a test to determine the sex of the baby?'

'No!' Princess Karine's loud protest alarmed them. 'I

don't want to know the sex of my baby until after he . . . after it's born. I shall love the baby whatever it is.'

'Of course you will, darling,' the Prince assured her. 'I'm sorry; I didn't mean to upset you. Please forget what I said about a son . . .'

As if she could! Jacky thought as she watched the royal pair holding hands like a couple of lovers after a quarrel.

'And now I think George should get some rest,' Carl suggested after a few minutes.

'I'll come back this afternoon, darling,' the Princess promised her husband.

Carl opened the door for her and she paused to look up at him and say, 'Thank you so much for offering your services with our daughters. I told them and they were delighted. Of course, we'll have to fit in with your medical commitments here, but you must let me make all the arrangements—hotels and so forth.'

'Of course.' The surgeon was smiling. Only Jacky knew how he really felt. He cast her a glance as he closed the door and she reflected that if looks could kill . . .

'Let's get these tests finished, Sister,' he ordered brusquely.

Towards the end of the morning there was a lull in the work and Madeleine came to tell them that she had made coffee. Jacky was pleased to take a break and joined the secretary in the small medical staff room off the reception area. She was surprised to see that they had a visitor.

'Glad you could make it, Matthew,' Carl greeted the young man. 'Let me introduce our Nursing Sister, Jacky Diamond; this is Matthew Brearley, one of the candidates I interviewed yesterday.'

Madeleine poured out coffee from a silver percolator into large Wedgwood breakfast cups. She smiled as she handed a cup and saucer to the young man. 'What brings you to this part of the world? I detect from your voice that you're English.'

'Quite right. I've been doing scientific research for the

past year—attached to an American university. Now I can either go back to England or travel some more. This is why I want to get this job in Reichenstein.' He smiled across at the surgeon who would make the decision and was rewarded with a nod of approval.

'You certainly seem to have the right qualifications and background for the job,' Carl began carefully. 'But then so have many of the other candidates. This is why I've offered you a preliminary job here for your summer vacation. We have to be so careful about our personnel in medical research. You understand that your BSc degree will not permit you to undertake medical cases here unsupervised, but you'll be a great help in our small laboratory. So long as you're willing to be our general dogsbody for a few weeks and won't expect to be automatically offered the Reichenstein post then I think the situation will be mutually agreeable.'

'You've been most helpful, sir. I had no idea what I was going to do during the vacation. I'm glad you agreed to take me on. I've brought all my papers with me.' Matthew Brearley handed the surgeon a folder of documents.

'Thanks,' said Carl as he placed the folder on a small table beside him. 'Just a formality, you understand.'

Jacky had been studying the young man during his exchange with Carl and noticed that he was extremely nervous. He must want the Reichenstein job very badly, she thought. I hope the boss doesn't keep him stringing along as a dogsbody only to disappiont him at the end. But then nothing would surprise me about the arrogant Dr Harvey, she reflected bitterly. The young man was pushing a hand through his unruly brown curly hair and hanging on the boss's every word.

'I'm going to show Matthew round the medical wing,' the surgeon told her when they had finished their coffee. 'You can take the afternoon off. I shan't be needing you. But come back this evening to help me with the Prince. He'll need to spend another night down here.'

*   *   *

The afternoon sun shone down brilliantly on the rose garden. Jacky had decided to take a book down to the lake and spend her off-duty stretched out on the grass. She was surprised to find that there were wicker garden chairs beside the water. There was even a small table obviously used for royal picnics. She spread herself in a large armchair with the sun full on her face and arms for maximum suntan effect, adjusted her sunglasses to deflect the rays and began to read. It was an enthralling book—a mystery story that she had bought at Heathrow airport on her way over—and she was dying to find out how it ended. Strangely enough, the more she became interested the more she relaxed and the sleepier she became. Little by little her eyes closed and the book slipped from her fingers on to the grass.

How long she had been asleep she didn't know as she awoke with a start. The sun was beginning to slide lower in the blue cloudless sky and her skin felt hot and dry.

'I hope you creamed your skin before you came out here.' The deep male voice took her by surprise. Carl was standing in front of her, obliterating the rays of the sun. The bright light on his head made the black hair shine with a striking lustre.

'How long have you been standing there?' she asked, annoyed that he should find her in such an inelegant position.

'Long enough,' was his cryptic reply. 'I hadn't the heart to waken you.'

'Do you need me back at the house?' she asked quickly, gathering her book from where it had fallen at her feet.

'No; take your time. Everything's under control.' He stepped forward and drew up a chair beside her, easing himself into it with smooth movements. 'You've chosen a beautiful spot out here. What are you reading?' He leaned across to read the title on the spine of her book. 'So you like mysteries, I see.'

I like solving them . . .' Jacky stopped and glanced

warily at his face.

'Obviously,' he commented in a neutral tone. 'But let me give you a word of advice, Sister Sherlock Holmes; don't probe too deeply into affairs that don't concern you. You could get your fingers burned.'

She breathed in deeply. 'I presume you're referring to the Chris Douglas case. Well, let me tell you, I think it does concern me. I was very . . . er . . . fond of Chris. Besides which, I don't like to see things swept under the carpet. There's been an obvious cover-up, and you were in charge of the situation . . .'

'As I told you,' Carl interjected evenly, 'don't probe too deeply. You read the coroner's verdict in the press.'

'But supposing some other innocent young student should find himself in the same situation? I want to see that this sort of thing isn't repeated,' Jacky flung at him heatedly.

'It could never happen again,' he told her solemnly. 'You must trust me, Jacky.'

She stared into the dark, sincere eyes and wondered how she could ever doubt him. He was the most disturbing man she had ever met; impossible to understand the depths of his personality, but when he looked at her like this she believed every word he said.

He leaned forward and touched her lips lightly with his own. It was a caressing, soothing feeling, light as a butterfly's wing, but it stirred something deep inside her. He put out his strong sensitive hand and stroked the side of her cheek.

'My poor Jacky,' he murmured. 'Don't torture yourself.'

His fingers remained against her cheek for mere seconds, but the memory lingered on as they walked back over the well kept lawn. He left her outside the medical wing and she went to her room to change back into uniform. Her heart was still beating rapidly as she fixed the white cap on her head.

'Damn you, Carl Harvey,' she whispered to her reflection in the mirror. 'How dare you make me feel like this! But I won't be put off . . . I owe it to Chris to find out what really happened.'

CHAPTER FIVE

AWHOLE month has passed and Jacky had been so busy she found she had no time to brood over the Chris Douglas affair. It was always somewhere at the back of her mind, but there were other more immediate problems to contend with. She had helped the Princess to break the news of the expected baby to her little daughters, and as she had hoped, they were delighted. It had been up to Jacky to point out that their mother needed lots of rest to ensure that no harm came to the baby.

'Is that why you and Dr Harvey are going to take Helen and me to Niagara Falls?' asked the perceptive elder sister.

'Yes, Charlotte. Your mother can have a nice rest here in Detroit while we're away,' Jacky explained, glancing anxiously at her patient. She looks a bit peaky today, she noticed. Yes, the Princess is not her usual cheery self. She made a mental note that she would have a word with Carl about her that evening.

It was late in the day before she had an opportunity to speak to her boss in private. They were both clearing up the medical wing at the end of a busy day when Jacky broached the subject of Princess Karine.

'I agree with you; I've decided to call in an obstetrics colleague,' Carl told her as he stacked a pile of case notes by the filing cabinet. 'I was going to examine the Princess tomorrow anyway, so I've asked Dr Jim Gregory to come over He's one of the top specialists in obstetrics.'

'But does the Princess know he's coming?' Jacky asked quickly, remembering her insistence on utmost secrecy.

'Not yet.' The surgeon gave a boyish grin and sank down in his chair, waving towards another chair with an impatient gesture. 'Take the weight off your legs while we plan what we're going to say to her.'

'What *we're* going to say?' she queried as she lowered herself into the soft leather seat. 'Do I take it you want me in on the task of persuading Her Royal Highness? She won't like it, you know.'

'That's where you come in, Jacky. She'll listen to you. You must tell her that it's in her own best interest; that we'll do our utmost to preserve secrecy.' Carl giving her the benefit of one of his most winning smiles.

She stared back at him as she recognised the wheedling tone he always used when he wanted to get round her.

'And when am I supposed to convert the Princess to your way of thinking?' she asked in a cool voice. Really, the man was impossible!

'We're having dinner with the Prince and Princess this evening . . .'

'We are?'

He ignored her interruption. 'That would be an excellent time to discuss it. Perhaps after dinner when you ladies retire to the Princess's room while the gentlemen drink their port and smoke a cigar . . .'

'Good heavens! It's not going to be so formal, is it? You might at least have told me about it.'

'It's only a normal dinner in a royal household. The Princess invited us this morning. I'm surprised she didn't mention it to you. I accepted her invitation on behalf of both of us,' Carl said casually.

'And supposing I'd had a previous engagement?' Jacky queried coldly.

'You would have had to cancel it,' he informed her glibly. 'After all, a royal command is a royal command. To be honest, I wanted to be sure you wouldn't wriggle out of it . . .' he began as a wicked smile spread over his handsome face.

'Wriggle out of it?' she exploded angrily. 'Why should I want to do that?'

'To avoid me,' he stated in a matter-of-fact voice. 'Don't deny that's what you've been doing lately.'

'I don't deny it.' Her eyes flashed dangerously as she stared at him. 'I find it difficult to be with a man who won't give me a straight answer to my questions.'

'I'm sorry you feel like that,' he replied evenly. 'Perhaps you would prefer to leave this job. I could easily appoint someone else.'

'No, I like the job,' she put hastily. 'And I'm very attached to all our patients. I've tried not to let my . . . er . . . involvement with Chris Douglas spill over into my professional relationship with you, Carl . . .'

'And you've succeeded,' he put in quickly. 'We have an excellent relationship here in the medical wing. I would be happier if we could get together off duty, that's all. I find that an occasional night out helps to iron out a few differences and problems. Madeleine always enjoys having dinner with me.'

'I know; she told me.'

Carl was puzzled by the bitterness in her voice and wondered why she disliked his secretary. Will I ever understand women? he asked himself as he began filing away the medical case notes. 'Meet me outside the royal apartments at eight,' he told Jacky in a brusque, no-nonsense voice.

'Yes, sir,' she replied. 'Do you mind if I go up to my room now? I need to choose something to wear.'

'Wear that cream suit—the one you had on the night we went to Mario's.' He was looking at her over the top of his files. Her cheeks flushed at the thought that he had remembered their candlelit dinner and she stood up quickly to hide her confusion. 'Run along and make yourself beautiful, and let your hair down for once,' he added with a mischievous grin.

Jacky was out of the door before he could see her face. As she hurried along to her room she reflected again that the man was impossible! He had a way of manipulating her that was so infuriating. This was another reason why she had been avoiding him off duty . . . because he could twist her round his little finger, and this was the last thing she wanted. She wanted to remain cool and detached, and it was becoming more and more difficult. The less she saw of him the better . . .

He was waiting for her outside the royal apartments promptly at eight o'clock. Her heart missed a beat as she saw that he was wearing a dark tuxedo jacket which made him look even more like the film star doctor that her young patient Julie had swooned over. The crisp white dress shirt highlighted his summer tan and the tailored grey pinstripes seemed moulded to the muscles of his long legs. He stepped forward to meet her, a wide smile accentuating the rugged character lines of his face.

'You look lovely, Jacky,' he told her warmly. 'And I approve of the hair.' He reached out to touch a few strands of her blonde tresses.

If he only knew! she thought, as she remembered the hectic hour she had spent with the shampoo and conditioner, not to mention the hair-dryer! She resented the fact that a casual suggestion from the great man that she should let down her hair had sent her into a frenzy of activity. True, I could have twined it back into a chignon, she reflected, but Carl wouldn't have liked it like that . . . and I may as well put him in a good mood for the evening.

She accepted his arm as he rang the bell. Seconds later they were ushered into the royal sitting room and offered glasses of champagne. The Duchess was already seated by the ornate marble fireplace, and her face broke into a smile when she recognised her doctor and his pretty young Nursing Sister.

'Come over here, Carl,' she requested in her quavering voice. 'My son will be along presently, so you can both talk to me. I've seen no one except the servants all day long. Why didn't you come to see me?'

'I've been very busy today, ma'am,' the surgeon replied in a deferential voice. 'But if I'd thought for one minute that you required my medical help . . .'

'Oh, stop being so formal, my boy!' the Duchess put in. 'It's not so long since I used to read you a bedtime story. You had time for me then, didn't you? And do you remember the time that I took you and George . . .'

'Maman!' remonstrated the Prince, coming over from the doorway to rescue his friend. 'I don't think Carl is interested in travelling down memory lane this evening.'

'Oh, but I find it fascinating. Do go on,' the surgeon replied hastily, as he reflected that a few minutes of his time would ensure that the old lady would relax, which was a good thing in view of her state of health.

The Prince turned his attention to Jacky as he admired her suit. 'It's so nice to see you out of uniform, Sister. I hope you will wear informal clothes when you take the girls to Niagara.'

'We are going to discuss all that later,' put in the Princess. 'Jacky and I are going to have a long tête-à-tête about clothes, the hotel, the car and so on. You don't need to worry about it, George.' She smiled at Jacky in a conspiratorial way. 'The main thing is that the Princesses should go unnoticed. I want you to pass for an ordinary family on a sightseeing jaunt. Do you think that's possible?'

'We'll try our best,' Jacky assured her. She had been watching Carl as he chatted with the Duchess and reluctantly admiring the way he had the old lady hanging on his every word.

'Let's go in to dinner,' the Princess suggested, leading the way through a carved archway into the opulent dining room.

Carl gave his arm to the Duchess to help her rise from her seat. The Prince walked in between his wife and Jacky, commenting that it was to be a very informal dinner.

'Only the five of us this evening. It's such a pleasure to have a quiet night at home. I have to attend so many functions out here that I rarely have time for my family.'

Prince George sat down at the head of the table with the Princess on his right and Jacky on his left. Carl was seated beside her and the Duchess sat down opposite him, still intent on holding his attention. The old lady smiled as she saw her favourite starter appear on the table.

'*Vous aimez les escargots, mademoiselle*?' she asked Jacky, reverting to her mother tongue at the sight of the snails.

Jacky understood what was being asked. 'I'm not sure, ma'am,' she replied cautiously. 'I've never tried them.'

'They're delicious,' the Duchess told her, remembering to speak English again. 'Serve yourself, my dear.'

Tentatively, Jacky scooped a few shells on to her plate from the silver salver. She knew that Carl was watching her and as she turned to look at him she saw that he was holding back his laughter.

'Are you sure you wouldn't like some more?' he asked her solemnly as he took the silver serving spoons from her hand.

'Quite sure,' she replied, taking a deep breath before attacking the first shell. Surprisingly, she found that once she had got the hang of removing the *escargots* from their shells she enjoyed the taste.

'I see you're enjoying the garlic flavour,' commented her boss, a wicked gleam in his eye as he turned towards her.

'I agree with the Duchess—the *escargots* are delicious!' Jacky smiled up into his eyes, enjoying the approval she saw there. And there was something else—some indefinable emotion that made her pulses race. Hastily she turned back to the *escargots,* reflecting that this was another reason she avoided being with her boss in off-duty situations. He made her feel so dreadfully mixed up! One minute she was hating him and the next he made her feel like the only woman in the world who mattered. It was his wicked eyes, she decided unwillingly; those dark brown pools that drew her reluctantly towards them so that she found it difficult to tear her attention away . . .

'When do you take my granddaughters to Niagara?' the Duchess was asking Jacky in her thin wavering voice.

'Next week, ma'am,' Jacky replied dutifully.

'You will love the beautiful Falls. But you must take great care . . .' The grandmother continued in her cracking tones to offer advice on the care of her grandchildren, and the doctor and Sister nodded in agreement to reassure the old lady.

The main course of chicken in a creamy brandy sauce garnished with baby shrimps arrived and was served by one of the white-coated waiters. After this came a simple tossed salad and then cheese and fruit.

'Time for your little chat with the Princess,' whispered Carl under cover of the clatter of some plates.

Jacky glared at him, but her eyes gave her away. It was difficult to remain annoyed with a man like this, and he seemed fully aware of the effect he was having on her as he reached for her hand under the white linen tablecloth. She didn't return his squeeze, but her fingers felt quite limp when he let go.

'Would you care to come up to my apartment, Jacky?' the Princess asked, rising from the table. 'We'll leave the gentlemen to their port.'

Jacky half turned towards her neighbour and almost giggled as she saw him give her a big wink. So it was true—this little ritual actually did still take place, she realised, as she smiled at the Princess and prepared to follow her.

'Gisèle is here to take you to bed, Maman,' Prince George announced quickly, noticing that his mother was also leaving the table.

'Sometimes I feel like a child again,' grumbled the Duchess as she leaned on the arm of her old maidservant. 'I'm not tired, you know . . .'

'But it will be better if you rest now, ma'am,' the doctor put in quickly.

'If you say so, Carl,' the old lady grumbled as she shuffled towards the door.

Jacky followed the Princess along the corridor, up a flight of wide sweeping stairs to the gallery that led to the Princess's private apartment. It was very feminine—soft pastel pinks merged with dusky rose in the curtains and cushions of the sitting room—and the sofas were comfortable and cosily placed on either side of a stone fireplace. Huge red roses adorned a sculptured vase in the open fireplace which was lit up by concealed lighting in the chimney. The numerous table lamps with muted shades gave a gentle glow to the sitting area, and Jacky felt perfectly at ease as she sank down amid the cushions. It was a lived-in room, she noticed; the sort of place where a royal mother could relax with her children, far from the eyes of the public.

'Coffee, Jacky?' the Princess asked.

'Yes, please.' She glanced round the room and was relieved to see that they were alone. It would be easier to say what had to be said without the listening ears of the servants. She sipped the strong coffee from a tiny cup and reflected for as few moments on what she was going to say. Better get it right or Carl would be furious!

'How are you feeling?' she began tentatively in her on-duty Sister's voice.

'I'm a little tired—and I've had a slight dragging feeling for a couple of days, but it's nothing to worry about, I'm sure. Anyway, Carl is going to examine me tomorrow, so . . .'

'I wanted to discuss that with you,' Jacky interrupted hastily. 'Carl thinks it would be a good idea if you're seen by a leading obstetrician. After all, we can't be too careful, can we? We want only the best for our royal baby . . .'

'Impossible!' The Princess's voice rang out in agitation. 'No; think of the publicity! I'm going to stay here in my rooms until the baby is born. I don't want to see anyone but you Carl.'

'But Your Highness . . . Karine, you must put the baby's interest first. We'll do everything we can to ensure secrecy, but safety is more important. Carl wants you to have only the best medical care. We couldn't possibly leave you without adequate medical supervision when we go to Niagara, so he's taken the liberty of calling in the help of an eminent obstetrician, Dr Jim Gregory. You'll meet him tomorrow when you come down for your examination.' Jacky paused for breath as she watched her patient for a reaction to this announcement.

'You seem to have organised things completely,' the Princess stated in a flat voice. 'I presume Carl has consulted my husband.'

'But of course.' Jacky was glad she had asked her boss about this.

'George will agree to anything that Carl suggests,' the Princess observed drily. 'But supposing the news leaks out to the press and supposing I lose my baby? It would be just like last time . . .'

'And what if you lose the baby because you've avoided taking expert medical advice?' Jacky pleaded gently. 'Your pregnancy would have been a secret, but at what price?'

Princess Karine gave a deep audible sigh and leaned her dark head back against the sofa cushions. 'I can see I have no choice in the matter. I would never forgive myself if . . .' Her voice broke as she choked back a sob.

'You're going to have excellent medical care. Nothing will go wrong if you follow our advice,' put in Jacky hastily as she saw the tears in the Princess's eyes. 'And we'll arrange for Dr Gregory's visit to be kept quiet tomorrow.'

The Princess nodded and gave a brave smile. 'You are such a comfort to me, Jacky,' she acknowledged gratefully. 'It's good to have a woman I can talk to . . . Now, let's discuss your vist to Niagara. First of all, clothes . . .' She passed a lacy handkerchief over her eyes before applying her whole attention to the forthcoming expedition.

At the end of half an hour the basic plans had been arranged, and Jacky found herself looking forward to the prospect of a few days' sightseeing. She told herself the two little Princesses would be ideal chaperones. There was absolutely no reason why she need spend any time alone with her boss. It would be just like working in the medical wing—both of them intent on caring for their patients, with no time to think about each other . . .

Are you ready to rejoin the men?' Princess Karine asked.

Jacky came back to earth with a start, realising that she had been staring up at the ornate ceiling as she allowed her thoughts to dwell once more on the fragile relationship she enjoyed with her boss.

'Yes, let's go down,' she agreed quickly, gathering up the folder of notes she had taken concerning the Niagara trip.

The Princess gave her a curious look. 'You're a very lucky girl to be able to work for Carl. Don't you find him attractive? Everybody else does.'

'I never mix personal relationships with a professional situation,' Jacky told the Princess hurriedly, but a tell-tale blush stole over her face.

The Princess smiled to herself as she led the way over to the door. Another conquest for the delectable Carl, she thought, but the poor girl hasn't realised it yet. Either that or she's fighting hard not to fall for him. But why ever would she want to do that? He must be every woman's ideal man . . .

The men had retired to the royal sitting room when the ladies arrived downstairs. The loud guffaws of male laughter ceased as they opened the door and Carl and Prince George sprang to their feet deferentially.

Carl pulled a chair up near to Jacky as soon as the ladies were ensconced. 'Did you have an interesting chat?' he asked softly.

'There's no need to whisper, Carl,' put in the Princess wryly. 'I've agreed to see your Dr Gregory, but I shall be furious if the press hear about it.'

'Don't worry; they won't,' the surgeon assured her with a mischievous grin. 'I've made provision for a foolproof plan.'

The Princess looked puzzled, but Carl refused to divulge any information.

'The plan is so secret that I must refrain from telling anyone,' he whispered, his smiling face revealing how much he was enjoying the subterfuge.

It was only next morning that Jacky discovered what her boss was planning. As she went into Carl's office she was surprised to find a man in workman's overalls sitting at the desk.

'Who on earth . . .?' she began, but the strange man interrupted her.

'I came to mend the X-ray equipment,' he told her.

'But I didn't know it was broken,' she faltered uneasily. There was something weird about the way the man was staring at her. Oh heavens, I hope he's not an intruder, she thought anxiously. And why is he sitting in Carl's chair?

'Jim, you old fraud!' The surgeon's deep voice had never been so welcome.

Jacky stared round as her boss hastily closed the door and advanced on the stranger with outstretched hand. 'I hope I haven't kept you waiting,' he was telling the unknown man in a voice full of friendly cordiality.

'Would you mind . . .?' Jacky began tentatively.

'Sorry; I meant to get here before you,' her boss apologised. 'Sister Jacky Diamond—Dr Jim Gregory.'

She accepted the stranger's hand. 'So you're the obstetrician! What was all that about the X-ray equipment?'

'Cover, my dear girl,' Carl told her with a mischievous grin, and then, turning to his colleague, he asked, 'Did anyone spot you, Jim?'

'Not in these clothes. I drove round the back and parked the old car I've borrowed from one of my students. The security man had been told to expect a workman going to the medical wing, so there was no problem.' The obstetrician smiled at his colleague. 'You always enjoyed a touch of mystery, Carl. You certainly planned this manoeuvre very well. Not even Sister Diamond knew who I was.'

'Oh, Dr Harvey never tells me anything,' Jacky said pointedly. 'I'm always the last person to know what he's planning.'

'But isn't it difficult to work under such circumstances?' asked Dr Gregory ingenuously.

'Extremely.' Jacky found it hard to conceal the bitterness from her voice.

The obstetrician glanced from one to the other, wondering what kind of hornets' nest he was stirring up. Beneath their polite exterior those two are gunning for each other, he thought anxiously, but I can't imagine why.

Jacky was enjoying the look of sympathetic concern on Dr Gregory's face. Her first appraisal of him was that here was a man who, although high up in his medical field, had retained a down-to-earth approach that must endear him to his patients. He's not handsome in a classical sort of way, she mused, but there's something very attractive about the way he smiles. His eyes crinkle at the corners and I like the casual unruly fair hair—although that might be part of his disguise as a workman, she decided. Maybe he had it sleeked back when he plays the important consultant in Detroit . . .

'Do you think we could have some coffee while we discuss the Princess's case?' Carl asked abruptly. 'Madeleine hasn't put in an appearance yet, so you may as well make yourself useful.'

'Of course,' Jacky replied in a cool voice as she left the office.

It was clear, on her return with the coffee pot, that they had been discussing her, because the conversation stopped abruptly. Either that or there's something else they don't want me to know, she figured as she poured out the coffee and handed cups and saucers to the two doctors.

They drank their coffee as they discussed Princess Karine's medical history. Jacky was able to fill them in on the emotional state of the pregnant Princess as she told the doctors about her conversation of the previous evening.

'I'm glad you were able to persuade the princess to see me,' Dr Gregory observed. 'Carl told me that she might be unwilling.'

'She disagreed with the idea at first because she was afraid your arrival might provoke speculation about her condition,' Jacky told him.

'But how long does she intend to go on with this little charade? I mean, she must be getting bigger. How far on is she?' The obsterician was glancing at the notes.

'Eighteen weeks,' Carl supplied.

'But she's wearing loose summer dresses and it doesn't show,' smiled Jacky. 'She says she wants to stay in her apartment until after the baby is born. . .'

'Impossible!' Dr Gregory said heatedly. 'The woman must be made to see sense. Princess or no princess, she must do what's best for the baby.'

'Don't worry, we're working on it, Jim,' the surgeon told him quietly. 'Sister Diamond is excellent at getting her own way with the Princess. We can rely on her to get through the stubborn streak.'

'You're very lucky to have a Nursing Sister who's so competent.' Dr Gregory smiled at his colleague. 'I hope you value her help.'

Carl smiled back at him. 'Oh, I do; she's made herself totally indispensable,' was his cryptic reply.

Jacky avoided the smiling gaze of her boss which she knew had transferred itself to her. 'Would you like me to escort the Princess down here?' she asked quickly.

'That would be an excellent idea,' her boss replied, moving towards the door so that he could hold it open for her.

Such gallantry! she thought as she swept through. It's purely for effect in front of his colleague, was her rational explanation as she mounted the stairs to the royal apartments.

She found the Princess in a highly emotional state. She had slept badly and was in a bad temper.

'I've changed my mind,' she told Jacky abruptly. 'I have total confidence in Carl and I don't want to see anyone else.'

'But Dr Gregory is already here . . .' Jacky began.

'Then he'll have to go away again,' was the peevish response. 'He will of course be paid for his visit.'

'It's not a question of payment, Your Highness,' Jacky put in with ominous calm. Her use of the royal title was deliberate; to distance herself from her obstreperous patient and show her disapproval. 'In your own interest, you must allow the obstretrician to examine you.'

'I'll think about it,' the Princess said in a cool, haughty voice, adding vaguely, 'Perhaps tomorrow . . .'

'But it was extremely difficult for Dr Gregory to arrive here undetected. And he has other commitments . . .'

'Invite him to stay for a couple of days. Madeleine can arrange it. She's very efficient.' The Princess turned away and retreated to an inner room, leaving Jacky standing inside the royal entrance hall feeling helpless.

There was nothing she could do except return to the medical wing to report on the unexpected turn of events. To her relief the obstetrician showed no surprise whatsoever.

'This happens all the time with the rich and famous,' he observed blandly. 'I used to work in Hollywood, and I spent half my time waiting around for these spoilt dames.'

Jacky smiled at his description of the Princess as a spoilt dame! He had a delightful West Coast drawl that she found refreshing after her boss's clipped English public school accent.

'Sure, I'll stay for a few days if that's what they want. I've got a good deputy back at the hospital who'll take over. I'll give him a ring and tell him I'm tied up,' Dr Gregory announced easily.

'Come this way, sir . . . and then I'll organise a room for you.' Madeleine had been only too delighted to be put in charge of accommodating the American doctor and was now playing at perfect hostess.

'So it's business as usual, is it? Jacky enquired when she was left alone with her boss.

'Looks like it.' Carl was standing by the window, the mid-morning sun shining on his face. He turned to face her and smiled. 'It's frustrating to be defeated after all our plans. Maybe tomorrow . . .'

'I'm sorry I couldn't persuade the Princess . . .' she began, but he came swiftly round the desk and put his fingers gently over her lips.

'Hush, Jacky,' he whispered softly. 'You did what you could, and I appreciate it. Don't be discouraged by one little setback.' his fingers dropped to her chin and he tilted it upwards so that she was forced to look into the deep brown eyes.

For a few seconds their eyes met in a gaze of mutual sympathy. They had tried and failed, but there was always tomorrow, Jacky was thinking, but then her pulses began to race as she recognised something besides sympathy in Carl's eyes. She had seen that look before and she knew . . . she hoped . . . he was going to kiss her. As his lips bent toward hers she moved imperceptibly to meet them. His mouth felt warm and exciting; shivers of emotion ran through her as he put his hands on her shoulders and she smelled the tangy odour of his distinctive cologne.

'Thanks, Jacky,' she heard him say, and her senses returned as she realised that she had been standing in his arms with her eyes closed, wanting the delicious stolen moment to continue. She had no idea what he was thanking her for. It might be the kiss; unlikely! she thought as she pulled away hastily and made for the door. He's merely acknowledged that I'm good at my job. I hope he didn't feel me responding to him just now! She was appalled at the thought, and spent the rest of the day avoiding being alone with her boss.

It wasn't difficult. After the morning clinic they went their separate ways. Jacky had a well-earned afternoon

off duty, while Carl spent the rest of the day
entertaining his medical colleague. Their paths didn't
cross once and Jacky told herself she was relieved. She
spent the afternoon shopping in the big Detroit
department stores. She wasn't exactly looking for
clothes for her Niagara trip, she told herself, but was
delighted when she found a few interesting items to
brighten up her wardrobe. After all, it wouldn't do to
look shabby beside the debonair Dr Carl Harvey.

CHAPTER SIX

ALL BUT emergency calls were cancelled in the medical wing next morning when the Princess told Jacky that she would submit to an examination by the obstetrician.

'I'm sorry I was so difficult yesterday,' Princess Karine admitted to her Nursing Sister as they went down the wide staircase together. 'I felt dreadful, and I was afraid that something would happen to the baby if I had an examination.'

'You need have no fears about any harm coming to the baby,' Jacky assured her hurriedly. 'Dr Gregory is a most experienced obstetrician.'

She ushered her royal patient into the medical wing, which was empty except for the two doctors. None of the other staff had been informed of what was going on. After the initial greetings and introduction, Jacky prepared the Princess for examination. As the two men came into the main cubicle, she held her patient's hand, sensing the fear and apprehension that lay behind the Princess's cool expression.

As the examination progressed, Jacky could see that both doctors were worried about something. She was too involved with calming her patient to be able to take part in scrutinising the internal anatomy which seemed to be causing the problem. Both men excused themselves for a few minutes and Jacky could hear their subdued voices in the outer office.

'What's happening?' the Princess asked her. 'Why don't they tell me what's wrong?'

'It may be nothing important,' Jacky began as she tried to sound convincing while playing for time. 'Whatever it is, you may be assured that . . .'

'Karine, we've decided you need some special treatment,' Carl said gently as he returned, a bright professional smile on his face. 'You seem to have developed some cervical incompetence during the last few weeks. In other words, there's a certain slackness at the neck of the womb which might be dangerous,' he explained quickly. 'So we've decided to put in a suture to ensure that the neck of the womb remains closed until you reach full term. Now there's nothing to worry about, my dear,' he soothed as he began to scrub his hands.

A Shirodkar suture, Jacky thought with relief. There'll be no danger of losing the baby if the cervix is closed. She had seen the method used often in the treatment of repeated spontaneous abortion, and it had always proved effective. This was probably why she lost the other babies, she deduced. There must be a weakness of her cervix which develops as the pregnancy progresses. Her hands flew rapidly over the necessary equipment, checking that everything was ready for the two doctors.

She stood beside her patient as the Shirodkar suture was being inserted, explaining in a soothing voice what was happening.

'It's rather like a purse string,' she told her wide-eyed patient, who was hanging on to her hand as if her life depended on it. 'It's drawn around the neck of the womb so that the baby can't slip out.'

'You're being very brave,' Carl said as he paused to watch his patient's reaction. 'Almost finished . . .'

The Princess lay very still at the end of the treatment. She seemed exhausted by the operation and the trauma of realising that something had actually gone wrong with the pregnancy.

'Thank you all very much,' she whispered in a quiet voice. 'I'm glad you found out what was wrong. I had a feeling that all wasn't well, but I was reluctant to admit it.'

'It's always best to take the bull by the horns, Your Highness,' Dr Gregory said in a cheerful voice. He was only too relieved that he had been able to make his royal patient see sense. Sometimes they were much more difficult than this, he mused as he flashed the Princess a smile of approval. 'And now, if you'll excuse me, Carl, I must get back to the hospital. I'll give you a ring to find out how things are going,' he added as he disappeared into the outer corridor.

Jacky stayed in the medical wing for a couple of hours until the Princess had fully recovered. When she accompanied her patient back to the royal apartments, Princess Karine requested her to stay on and have lunch with her.

'Nothing very much—just a light lunch on a tray in my sitting room,' Her Highness elaborated. 'I feel I need to talk to someone.'

'I'd love to,' said Jacky in a reassuring voice. It was good to see that the Princess was her usual friendly self again. She hadn't enjoyed being treated like one of the servants during yesterday's contretemps. 'I'd better tell Carl where I am,' she added hastily. 'He likes to keep tabs on me.'

'I'm sure he does. You can use my internal phone,' the Princess told her as she lay back amid the soft cushions of her favourite sofa. 'Louise, you can serve lunch now—Sister Diamond is joining me.'

After a second request in French the maid departed to the kitchen, while Jacky picked up the ornate telephone to ring her boss. She smiled as she noticed that the pseudo-antique brass instrument had been specially designed to blend in with the Sheraton-style table on which it was standing.

Her boss seemed pleased that she had been invited to lunch when she got through to him. 'That's fine, Jacky. Keep up the good work,' he told her. 'And make sure the Princess rests all the afternoon.'

'Of course . . .' She hesitated. 'When do you need me back in the medical wing?'

'There's nothing urgent at the moment. I'm going to work on some papers with Madeleine this afternoon. I'll ring you if something comes up.' The line went dead, and Jacky returned the heavy phone to its cradle feeling slightly deflated. She was beginning to find that she disliked spending long hours away from Carl. Even when he snapped at her—as he often did—it gave her a thrill. And she loved working with him . . . side by side, leaning over a patient, both intent on pooling their medical ideas . . .

'I hope you like salmon.' The Princess's voice broke in on her thoughts.

'Yes, I do,' she said hastily as she turned her attention to the tray which Louise was setting down in front of her. There were tiny slices of wafer-thin brown bread elegantly arranged beside a plate of fresh salmon and cucumber. In one corner of the silver tray was a crystal dish of strawberries and kiwi fruits. 'This looks delicious,' she told her hostess.

The princess smiled and told her maid that they wouldn't require her for a couple of hours. She chatted easily to Jacky as they lunched, seemingly relieved that she had faced up to the ordeal of the medical examination and come out with flying colours.

'I like Dr Gregory,' she told Jacky. 'But I would never have admitted to his examination if Carl hadn't been there. Carl gives me such confidence—don't you find that?'

'Yes, I do,' Jacky replied carefully. 'He's an excellent doctor.'

'He's the best. I would trust him with my life,' the Princess stated boldly. 'That was why I could never understand how anyone could doubt his integrity . . .' Her voice trailed away as she watched Jacky's surprised reaction. 'Oh, maybe I shouldn't have said that,' she added quietly.

Jacky took a deep breath. 'Who doubted his integrity?' she asked blandly.

'Well, it was something George told me. There was an unfortunate incident when he was director of that pharmaceutical firm. A medical student died and the whole thing had to be hushed up. The investigation is still going on, I believe but Carl got out of it as quickly as he could. That was when George offered him this job. He'd been planning to ask him to run our new medical project and it just meant that we had his services earlier than expected. From our point of view it was ideal . . .'

The Princess's voice droned on, extolling the virtues of her favourite surgeon, but Jacky wasn't listening. So that was what happened, was it? she mused, and a shiver of apprehension ran through her veins. What did the Princess mean when she said that Carl had got out of it as quickly as he could? Was he sacked? Did he resign? And the investigation is still going on . . .

'Are you all right, Jacky? You've gone quite pale.'

She heard the Princess's voice as if in a dream. 'Yes, I'm fine,' she replied quickly. 'What were you saying?'

'I was saying that Carl is incapable of subterfuge. If he could have helped with the investigation I'm sure he would have. But I'd rather you didn't mention it to him. I believe he doesn't like to talk about it,' the Princess concluded rapidly. 'Let's talk about your trip to Niagara Falls.'

They were both relieved by the change of subject and spent a fruitful afternoon planning the entire expedition, from the number of hotel rooms required to the suitability of jeans versus dresses for the small Princesses. It was decided to take one of the maids, and Jacky suggested Julie, the young girl who had visited the morning clinic at the beginning of her stay.

'She's very intelligent and I would find her a great help. She's only working as a maid until it's time to go back to college,' Jacky informed the Princess. She decided that nothing would be served by divulging the girl's medical history. The anorexia nervosa seemed to be under control, and one of the contributory factors to Julie's dismenorrhoea was her boredom with the job of dusting the furniture. Jacky was sure that the girl would perk up if she was given something interesting to do.

'I'll leave the choice of maid to you, Jacky. If the girl is suitable then take her with you. And I think you should have one of the chauffeurs . . .'

'No, that's not necessary,' Jacky put in hastily, remembering her boss's dislike of uniformed men standing to attention. He couldn't wait to get rid of our royal chauffeur when we went out to Mario's, she reflected with a wry grin. 'It would only draw attention to the Princesses,' she stated logically.

'I suppose you're right.' Princess Karine paused and looked thoughtful before she came up with an idea. 'Why don't you take that young scientist who's helping Carl in the laboratory? I'm sure he wouldn't mind sharing the driving with Carl for a few days. What's his name?'

'You mean Matthew Brearley, don't you? Yes, he gets on well with Carl and he doesn't seem to mind what he does so long as he gets paid—oh, I didn't mean that in a derogatory sense,' Jacky added quickly when she saw the Princess's amused smile. 'I simply meant that, like all young men, he's always short of cash. I think that's why Carl took pity on him and gave him a job for the summer. He's considering offering him a post in the Reichenstein project.'

'Yes, I believe George mentioned it. Well, now's the time for Carl to assess his character in a leisure situation. It's often easier to find out what makes a person tick when they're relaxed,' the Princess stated with a wise shake of her head.

Jacky promised to discuss it with her boss as she gathered up her file and prepared to leave. There was so much to be done before the journey that she wanted to get on with it. When she was quite sure that the Princess had everything she needed, she excused herself and made her way to the medic 1 wing.

The swing doors opened noiselessly as she hurried through them. She could see that Carl's door was partly open and she could hear voices from inside. Something made her pause on the threshold instead of going straight in.

'I'm glad you came with me, Madeleine. I couldn't have coped without you,' Jacky heard her boss say in a deep, sincere voice. She stood quite still outside the door, half of her wanting to make her presence known and the other half holding back.

'It was the least I could do.' Madeleine's soft dulcet tones penetrated the half-open door. 'After all, you've been so good to me over the years. We've both had our problems, and it's been great to have a shoulder to cry on . . .'

'And someone you could pour out your troubles to . . .'

Jacky froze against the wall as she heard the emotion in Carl's voice. There was silence inside the office now. What are they doing? she wondered anxiously. Has he taken her in his arms? How on earth can I beat a silent retreat out of here . . .

'We'd better get on with some work.'

She held her breath at the boss's words and then breathed a sigh of relief as she heard Madeleine's typewriter start tapping. She counted to ten and then, under cover of the noise of the keys, she stole over to the swing doors. Swinging them as noisily as she could, she called out,

'Anyone here?' before marching over to Carl's office.
As she looked at the hard-working pair, he bent over the
filing cabinet and his secretary tapping away at the
typewriter, she decided she must have imagined the
tender little interlude. 'Could we discuss the
arrangements for Niagara?' she asked her boss brightly.

The surgeon hesitated. 'Well, we're rather busy, but I
suppose it's got to be done some time. Madeleine, could
you take your work back into your office for the
moment?'

The tapping stopped and the secretary turned to look
at the Sister. 'If you think I'm going to be in the way I'll
most certainly go back to my room,' she said evenly, as
she began to gather up her things. 'I take it that you
won't need me to accompany you on this . . . er . . .
expedition, Carl?' she added pointedly.

'You'll be far more use holding the fort here,' her
boss replied smoothly, and was rewarded with a faint
smile from his loyal secretary. 'Now, what did you want
to discuss, Jacky?' he asked, when they were alone.

Jacky outlined the plans, being very careful to ask his
advice about Julie and Matthew. She didn't want to be
accused of insubordination again. Carl thought it was a
good idea to take the two young people and reiterated
the Princess's opinion that it would be a good
opportunity to get to know Matthew.

'He seems a very amenable sort of young man,'
surgeon volunteered carefully. 'What do you make of
him, Jacky? It's OK, you can speak freely; there's no
one here this afternoon except Madeleine. I gave him
the afternoon off.'

Was that so that you could have a cosy time with
Madeleine? she wondered, but quickly put the thought
out of her head. There was no point becoming involved
in her boss's personal affairs, she told herself as she
tried to concentrate on his query about Matthew.

'He works hard; he's good-tempered, reliable, and

I like him,' she told her boss quickly.

'You don't find him . . . er . . . quiet?' Carl asked her.

She frowned. 'Only when he's working—and that can be a good thing.'

'Of course,' he agreed. 'Well, if you've nothing more to discuss, I suggest you go off duty. I'd like to finish my work with Madeleine.'

Jacky gave her boss a bright smile. 'Yes, I mustn't take up any more of your time,' she murmured quietly. The sound of the typewriter had stopped in the secretary's office and she could hear the clickety-clack of stiletto heels advancing in their direction. There was no point staying on where she wasn't required, she reflected as she passed Carl's secretary in the doorway.

The next few days passed in a flurry of preparations. The little Princesses were beside themselves with excitement at the prospect of their Niagara holiday and phoned down to the medical wing several times on some pretext or other.

'Do I need to take my inhaler, Dr Harvey?' Helen asked on one occasion.

The surgeon smiled and, cupped his hand over the mouthpiece, he said to Jacky, 'It's Their Royal Highnesses again—junior variety. Pop up and check on inhalers for Helen, will you?'

Jacky smiled and nodded as her boss resumed speaking.

'Sister Diamond is coming up to see you, Helen,' he told the young Princess.

'Thank you so much,' was the demure reply.

Carl grinned at Jacky as he put the phone down. 'Her Royal Highness the Princess Helen will see you now,' he told her in an exaggerated tone of voice. 'Take some more ointment and dress her arms, while you're up there. It will save any further disruption down here.'

'Will do,' Jacky smiled as she swung out through the

corridor.

The last couple of days were spent in packing cases and arranging for medical cover during their absence. Dr Gregory had agreed to make himself available if necessary, but he stressed that he was not going to go to any great lengths to conceal his identity in an emergency.

'I'm not going through that mad charade again,' he had told Carl. 'If the Princess needs me she'll have to risk the story leaking out. Anyway, I think she's got an excellent chance of carrying this baby to full term, so I don't know why she doesn't announce her pregnancy. Rumours are bound to start soon, if she keeps to her apartment all the time.'

Carl had agreed with his colleague, but insisted that they respect the Princess's wishes a little longer. Jacky was pleased that the obstetrician was optimistic about her patient. It made it so much easier to leave her in his care when they left the royal household.

As the car rolled down the drive with Matthew at the wheel, Jacky breathed a sigh of relief. It had been like planning an expedition to climb Mount Everest, she reflected, and smiled at the thought.

'You look happy,' Carl said over the heads of the little Princesses.

'I'm relieved we've got away at last. There were times during the last few days when I never thought we'd make it,' Jacky told him.

'You've been great,' her boss replied quietly.

'Thank you.' She turned away and stared out of the window. It wasn't often Carl paid her a compliment, she reflected, but when he did it really meant something to her. She was beginning to value his approbation more and more.

The two little girls sitting between them on the back seat began to squirm and fidget before long. There was a huge tailback of cars waiting at the immigration post, and the Princesses wanted to get going. They weren't used to being held up like this. In the royal limousine they would have received VIP treatment.

'This is the price we have to pay for taking you on an ordinary holiday,' Carl explained gently. 'You wanted to see what life is like outside, so you'll just have to be patient. And when it's our turn to show our passports I'd like you to leave all the talking to me.'

The Princesses agreed to behave themselves at the border, and they were quiet and still when Carl filled out the immigration papers necessary to cross over into Canada. The officials stared in amazement when they realised who the little girls were, but as all their papers were in order they were allowed to move on quickly.

'I hope they don't start talking to anyone about our visit,' said Carl as the car sped across Ambassador Bridge towards Windsor.

'Look at the river!' Charlotte squealed excitedly as she pointed out of the window. 'Can you see the big ships, Helen?'

Both girls had scrambled on to Carl's lap as they gazed out at the spectacular river view. He held on to them until the river was out of sight. Then he insisted they sat down again on the seat while he described some of the sights they were going to see at Niagara.

Jacky smiled to herself as she listened to his now familiar deep voice. He would make a perfect father, she thought. I wonder why he isn't married—or maybe he is! The thought had never occurred to her before. Just because there was no Mrs Harvey out here it didn't mean that one didn't exist. He might have some dear little wife waiting for him back home. But where is his home? she wondered. She knew his medical work had been based in London, but that didn't mean he lived there. Strange, I know so little about him, she thought as she cast her eyes in his direction. He was concentrating all his energies on entertaining the

Princesses, and they were living it.

He's captivated them, she recognised, and then admitted to herself unwillingly that she too felt the same way about him. In spite of everything he may have done I can't help falling for him, she thought. A feeling of guilt swept over her as she thought about poor Chris. Her reason for coming out here had been to solve the mystery of his death, she reminded herself, and here she was mooning over the very man who could help her but refused to do so. It was all such a muddle . . .

She closed her eyes and lay back against the soft leather of the seat. The car wasn't as opulent as the royal limousine, but it was still extremely comfortable, she reflected as she allowed Carl's words to drift over her. He was explaining to the Princesses how the water thundered over Niagara Falls. 'It's falling, falling, deep, deep down to the depths . . .' she heard him say before the rhythm of his voice sent her to sleep.

She dreamed that she too was falling like the water into a deep whirlpool where she was tossed hither and thither. A man was standing on a path beside the river and she tried to cry out to him. He was staring at her, and she recognised who it was, but he wouldn't help her. He stood by with a mocking smile while she floundered in the water. In her dream she called his name.

'Carl!' As the strangled cry broke loose she woke with a jerk.

'Jacky, what's the matter?' Carl was all concern as he leaned across to take hold of her hand.

'I don't know,' she faltered. 'I think I must have fallen asleep.' She shivered as she saw the face from her dream only inches from her own. But this was a kind and gentle face, not sinister and hostile as she had imagined in her dream. There was genuine sympathy in those languid brown eyes.

'You must have been very tired to fall asleep so

easily,' the surgeon said in his bedside-manner voice. 'You've been overworking recently. We'll pull up soon and have some lunch. Matthew, turn off at the next exit and we'll look for a little restaurant. I don't want to eat at one of the huge places on this road. Someone might recognise the Princesses and we'd get no peace . . .'

'But I wanted a hot dog!' wailed little Helen. 'I've never had a hot dog. And Maman said . . .'

'We'll get you a hot dog, if that's what you really want, but it will have to be somewhere off the beaten track,' Carl decreed firmly.

Matthew turned the car into a side road and they cruised along until they came to the outskirts of a small town. It was a sleepy-looking place. At first glance, Jacky had the impression that everything had closed down before she realised that it was the midday break. Most people were taking a leisurely lunch and no one was in a hurry. There was time to spare in this dear little town. Even the cat on the doorstep of the small restaurant was curled up asleep and didn't move as they stepped over him.

The Princesses were intrigued by the weird atmosphere of the interior and stared around them as Carl ushered them to a table. It was not the home-cooking type of restaurant he had hoped to find, but, at least they should be able to remain incognito in a place like this, he reflected. Apart from a young waitress who had emerged from the kitchen they were the only people in evidence.

The girl produced a menu and put it solemnly on the table in front of Carl. Helen, who was still clinging tightly to his hand, announced,

'I would like a hot dog, please.'

'You'd better let your daddy choose,' the waitress advised the little girl, oblivious to the amused smiles of her clients.

'He's not my daddy; my daddy is . . .'

'We'll have a hot dog for the little girl, right away,' Carl interrupted hurriedly. 'And the rest of us will have the home-made vegetable soup and the dish of the day.'

'Instantaneous decisions; that's what I like about you, sir,' Matthew commented with a friendly grin as the young waitress moved away back to the kitchen. He was sitting opposite his boss and looked more relaxed than usual in his red check sports shirt and faded blue jeans.

'Some decisions can be made instantaneously; things that are trivial, such as what to wear, what to have for lunch and so on aren't worth spending time on. But some big problems need long careful consideration,' the surgeon replied in a quiet, thoughtful voice. 'I think I agonise over important decisions as much as anyone. But then, in the end, you have to trust your own judgement and hope you've got it right.'

'What do you consider an important decision?' Julie asked in a nervous voice. It was the first time she had spoken to the great man in a social situation and she felt rather like a fish out of water. She had been thrilled when Jacky asked her to accompany them on this expedition—anything was preferable to being holed up in the royal mansion as a glorified cleaner! she had decided—but she wasn't quite sure of her place in the hierarchy here. It was as if she had been elevated too quickly from back-stairs maid to confidante.

'That's a difficult question,' the surgeon smiled. He had been wondering if the girl had a tongue in her head any more. She had been talkative enough as a patient in the medical wing, but she hadn't said a word in the car. It was a relief to see that she was enjoying herself, he thought, and it was also good to see that she was prepared to eat a good lunch. It looked as if her anorexia nervosa days were over. Yes, she's definitely put on some weight since I first saw her, he noticed with approval.

'I agree it's a difficult question.' Jacky spoke up in a firm voice as she turned to look at her boss. 'But we all have to make difficult decisions at some time in our lives. I think Julie wanted the benefit of your opinion on what constituted a major decision. I mean, what would you agonise over?' she finished with an embarrassed smile. A slow flush spread over her face as she realised that her intense tone had betrayed her deep involvement with this man. What had started out as a lighthearted conversation was turning into an inquisition again.

The surgeon focused his gaze upon her and his eyes were hard as steel. 'Matters of life and death; whether to keep a patient on a life-support machine or switch it off; whether to tell a terminally ill patient he had only weeks to live; whether to operate and extend the life of a patient even though the quality of his life will be poor.' He paused and took a deep breath before continuing. 'When you have to make decisions like this, everyday problems appear trivial.'

The room had gone quiet. Only the sound of water trickling from a bizarre plastic fountain in the centre of the room disturbed the silence. Seconds elapsed before the tension was broken by one of the Princesses.

'Look at the cat!' Helen cried in an excited voice as she pointed towards the corner of the room.

Jacky looked in the direction of the little girl's finger, relieved that the atmosphere had been dispelled. A brightly coloured plastic dustbin had been placed at the side of an ancient harmonium. It looked hopelessly incongruous, but what was even stranger was the fact that its lid was wired up to some mechanism which caused it to rise and fall intermittently, revealing the grinning face of a lifelike toy cat.

'I want to stroke it,' the small Princess announced, and was only prevented from rushing across the room by the arrival of her long-awaited hot dog.

The conversation was kept deliberately light and

frivolous throughout the meal, and Jacky could see that
Carl was trying hard to create a holiday atmosphere for
all of them. She made a conscious decision that she
would not interrogate her boss at the least opportunity,
because it was obvious that he wasn't going to be drawn
and there was no point in antagonising him. Far better
to wait for exactly the right moment, she told herself as
she bit into a delicious pear.

'That was a much better meal than I expected when
we first walked in here,' Carl remarked quietly.

Jacky agreed. The soup really had tasted as if it was
home-made and the dish of the day, which had proved
to be a Canadian variation of coq au vin, had been
excellent. Carl paid the bill and they all trooped outside,
carefully stepping over the somnolent feline again.

'Not quite Egon Ronay, but worth making a detour
for, wouldn't you say?' Carl remarked when they were
safely ensconced in their huge red station waggon.

'It was worth it to see the cats, both real and false,'
said Julie from the front of the car. She had enjoyed
getting to know the surgeon at lunchtime. Sister
Diamond had always been easy to get on with, she
mused, as the vehicle pulled out of the small car park,
but she had never known quite how to take Dr Harvey.
It was a relief to find he was so human under that suave
exterior. And he was so dishy! The young maid turned
to get a last glimpse of the unusual exterior of the
restaurant. On first arrival she had thought it looked
like the house in Alfred Hitchcock's film *Psycho*, but
now, with a good meal inside her and the afternoon sun
shining through the clouds, she thought it looked
positively inviting. Catching the eye of the surgeon, she
turned back hurriedly and gazed out of the front wind-
screen as she wondered if there was something going on
between those two on the back seat. They were always
either at each other's throats or smiling as if there was a
secret between them, she reflected.

They reached their hotel at Niagara-on-the-Lake in the late afternoon. The Princesses had slept for a couple of hours and were now refreshed and ready to be entertained, whereas Jacky was feeling decidedly tired. But she forced herself to remain patient with the little girls as she settled them into their room. It had been decided that they should have Julie sleeping in the room with them to be on hand if they required anything. But Jacky's room was right next door and there was a communicating door between the two rooms.

'Don't hesitate to call me if you need me,' Jacky told Julie as she retreated into her own room. Julie had promised to show the princesses round the mini-park that surrounded the hotel, and Matthew had offered to accompany them. As she closed the inter-connecting door, Jacky reflected that she had no qualms about relinquishing her charges for a short time. Matthew and Julie were proving to be a most helpful pair.

She crossed to the window and flung it wide open. The air-conditioning switched itself off automatically as she breathed in the early evening air. There was a strong scent of roses drifting up from the rose garden below. Her eyes caught sight of a small Oriental-style enclosure; there were little wooden bridges and an ornamental fishpond overshadowed by a brightly coloured gazebo. And in the slanting rays of the sun she could make out the figure of a man. Her heart beat just a little bit faster, as it always did when she saw Carl unexpectedly. His long-legged stroll was unmistakable as she watched from her vantage point on the balcony. He looked uncharacteristically tired, and her heart went out to him.

How he must hate me for hounding him! she thought with a guilty pang. If only he'd come clean . . . if only he'd tell me what I want to know. I could leave him alone then. And as soon as this assignment is over I'd go out of his life and never see him again . . .

And then she saw a tall stranger stepping out from the gazebo and approaching the surgeon. They began to talk earnestly together. It was almost as if Carl had been expecting the meeting. But both men kept glancing around nervously. Jacky closed the window and went back into her room. Whatever mystery she had stumbled upon, she knew her boss would be furious if he caught her spying on him.

CHAPTER SEVEN

THE MIGHTY roar of the thundering falls assailed
Jacky's ears as she opened the door of the car. Matthew
had parked down the hill as near to Niagara Falls as he
could get, and the little Princesses were hopping up and
down in excitement. Jacky took hold of Helen's hand
and cast an experienced eye over her patient. She had
been forced to spend part of the night soothing the
asthmatic child and she didn't want her to get too
excited so that her breathing became difficult again.

'I'll take care of Helen if you hold on to Charlotte,'
she told Carl as he stretched his long legs out of the
parked station waggon.

'Yes, ma'am,' he said easily. 'I don't think we need
Matthew and Julie for a couple of hours. Why don't the
pair of you go off and enjoy yourselves while we try to
look like Mr and Mrs Average out for the day with two
of their offspring.'

'That's very kind of you, sir,' Matthew acknowledged
pleasantly.

'Don't call me sir around here,' his boss ordered with
a boyish grin. 'I'm just your old friend
Carl—remember?'

The young man nodded. 'Well, come on, Julie. What
are we waiting for?' He took hold of the girl's arm and
pulled her away into the milling crowds.

'What it is to be young!' Carl commented with a
pseudo-wistful smile.

'You poor old thing,' Jacky said smiling. 'Do you
think you can stagger as far as the Falls?'

'You'll have to help me,' he told her as he tucked his
arm in hers.

The foursome made their way down the slope towards the rushing river that frothed and gurgled at the foot of the Falls.

'I don't think we're fooling anybody with this family pretence,' Carl whispered in her ear under cover of the girls' shrieks of delight. 'You look much too young to be a mother.'

'Then why do we keep it up?' Jacky queried, beginning to disentangle her arm from his.

'Don't do that,' he chided swiftly. 'I'm enjoying myself. Three beautiful young ladies to accompany; what more could I ask for!'

'You're in a good mood today,' Jacky observed as they rounded the corner and the full glory of the Falls came into view. 'Oh, isn't that breathtaking!' she breathed, coming to a dead halt on the pavement.

Crowds of sightseers were milling round, but Jacky felt as if she and Carl were the only people who were experiencing the magnetic impact of the majestic Falls. The morning sun was shining on the Falls at the other side of the river, in the United States, while over here, on the Canadian side, the combination of spray and sun had created a rainbow arc where the turbulent water cascaded over the edge.

'I want to go near the water!' cried Charlotte, tugging on Carl's hand.' Let's go to the edge of the Falls!'

'Would you like to go under the Falls?' the surgeon asked, and smiled at the wide-eyed approval of his suggestion.

They walked along the path high above the river towards the entrance to the underground tunnels. Across the broad sweep of the river, Jacky could see the tourists visiting the American Falls. As they tramped around the winding paths near to the water's edge the tourists looked like creatures from another planet in their bright yellow raincoats.

'We all have to wear those when we go under the

Canadian Falls,' Carl explained, and for the first time
the little Princesses began to look apprehensive.

Helen was clinging tightly to Jacky's hand as they
went down the stone steps into the dark, underground
cloakroom where the yellow raincoats were handed out.

'I don't want to wear one of those,' Helen began as
the cloakroom attendant endeavoured to find a raincoat
of suitable size for the little girl.

'You'll have to wear one, my dear,' the kindly man
told the Princess as he went down on one knee to slot
the raincoat over her arms. 'What's your name, dear?'

Jacky held her breath as the little Princess smiled and
said, 'Helen. We're here on holiday. My mummy
couldn't come with us because . . .'

'That's a perfect fit! Thank you so much,' Jacky
broke in quickly. 'Come along, Helen.'

They were all squeezed into a lift that took them even
further into the bowels of the earth. Jacky was pressed
up against Carl and she glanced up at him, thinking that
it would be difficult to recognise the eminent surgeon
under all that clobber! Only his eyes, surrounded by the
layers of yellow plastic, gave the show away. She turned
away and found herself under the scrutiny of a tall man
who was squashed againt the lift doors. He had insisted
on leaping in at the last minute even though the
attendant had declared that the lift was full. Jacky had
wondered why he was in such a hurry. The lift was
delivering its passengers every few minutes. There was
something about the way he held his head, sort of
slightly on one side . . .

Where have I seen him before? she pondered, realising with a start that the stranger was scrutinising Carl
now. Don't be so melodramatic! she told herself
quickly. The man had a perfect right to stare if he wants
to . . . and then she remembered him! It was the tall
stranger she had seen in the garden last night talking
to Carl. His waterproof cap was too small, she noticed,

and a stray wisp of ginger hair was sprouting out from
under it. She remembered that hair vividly. If she could
recognise the man why didn't Carl? The surgeon was
staring straight ahead, giving no sign of recognition.

The lift doors opened and the human contents spilled
out into the dark tunnel. Jacky could hear the
thunderous roar of the falls overhead.

'We're now under Niagara Falls,' the guide was
explaining in a loud voice to reach over the rhythmic
drone of the torrent.

Jacky suddenly realised that she had a little Princess
on either side of her and Carl was nowhere to be seen.
As the crowd of sightseers surged eagerly forward she
was swept into the dark tunnel, clinging tightly to her
charges. There was no possibility of turning round when
you were pushed along like flotsam in a maelstrom, she
reflected resignedly.

They paused at one of the vantage points and the
crowd thinned, some of the people going to watch the
water spilling down the hillside and others impatiently
continuing to the end of the tunnel. Jacky was pulled
towards the daylight by her little charges.

'Look at the water!' cried Charlotte as they stared out
at the mighty cascade. She tried to wriggle her hand free
from Jacky's but Jacky only tightened her grip.

Little Princess Helen was overawed at the spectacle
and remained silent as drops of spray were blown
against her face. She seemed relieved when Jacky turned
to go back into the tunnel.

They followed the rest of the group on to the final
vantage point, where they were able to walk out of the
tunnel on to a rocky promontory. There they could see
the whole of the Falls as they thundered down into the
whirlpools below. It was an impressive sight and Jacky
would have liked to linger on, taking in the sheer beauty
of this once-in-a-lifetime experience. But Helen had
begun to shiver, and Jacky was worried. It wasn't cold,

but there was a feeling of dampness in the air and it wouldn't do for the little Princess to catch a chill. She picked the little girl up and turned to go back into the tunnel.

Strong arms reached out to remove the child from her grasp. 'We seem to have lost each other,' said Carl in a calm voice as he cradled the small Princess in his arms.

'I thought you'd deserted us,' Jacky observed quietly.

He chose to ignore her remark, or else he didn't hear it over the thunder of the waterfall. He strode ahead cradling his precious charge and Jacky followed, clinging tightly to Charlotte's hand.

The day seemed surprisingly warm as they emerged from the underground caverns. Jacky blinked at the sunlight and welcomed the warmth that began to flood through her chilled bones.

'Hot dogs, I think!' Carl's suggestion was greeted with whoops of delight from the two little girls.

'We'll never be able to keep up this diet back at the royal mansion,' Jacky remarked as Carl shepherded his girls towards the edge of the pavement.

'They're on holiday,' he reminded her as they crossed over the busy road. 'They'll soon return to normality when we get back.'

There was a brittle falseness to his boyish behaviour today, Jacky reflected. It was as if he was trying to cover up for his strange behaviour under Niagara Falls. What had he been up to? she wondered as she followed him into a gaudy fast-food restaurant. Neon signs proclaimed that this was the place where you could buy the biggest hot dogs in Niagara. Jacky shuddered at the very idea and requested coffee only.

It was amusing to watch the Princesses trying to swallow their hot dogs, and Jacky turned to look at Carl. He too was grinning all over his face.

'We look like a couple of doting parents,' he remarked, reaching out to put his hand over hers on the table.

The feel of his fingers awakened a deep longing inside her. They had grown so far apart recently and there were so many obstacles preventing their relationship from blossoming, she reflected sadly. She stared up into his face and saw a strange, enigmatic expression that she had never seen before.

'But even doting parents need a little time to themselves,' he continued in that same soothing voice that was beginning to dispel all her fears again. 'Will you have dinner with me tonight, Jacky?'

'I thought I was going to—I mean, we all dined together last night, didn't we?' she replied carefully, as she willed herself to stay calm.

'I don't mean like last night,' he told her earnestly. 'That was sheer hard work; four adults struggling with two fractious children at the end of a long day . . .'

She laughed at his apt description. 'I agree with you there. It was pretty disastrous. So what do you suggest?'

'The girls can have a high tea in the early evening and after they're in bed, we'll go down to the Oak Room Restaurant and live it up a little. Matthew and Julie can call us if they want to. They won't mind baby-sitting. I can spot a budding romance there.' Carl was smiling lightheartedly now as if he didn't have a care in the world.

Jacky studied the deep crease of his wide aristocratic brow. It sounded too wonderful for words, but she didn't want to appear too eager. 'This Oak Room Restaurant; is it in the hotel?'

'Of course it is; and it's so much more luxurious than the all-day restaurant where we ate last night,' he told her.

She looked at the shining brown eyes and her pulses began to race. 'If it's in the hotel then it will be quite safe for us to leave the Princesses for an hour . . .'

'Or two,' Carl put in with a mischievous grin. 'As

I told you, Matthew and Julie will love baby-sitting for us.'

'You've persuaded me,' Jacky admitted, and the smile that broke out over her face betrayed her.

Carl squeezed her hand before turning his attention back to his charges. 'Aren't you going to finish those?' he asked with a whimsical smile.

By the end of the afternoon, the Princesses were becoming tetchy and difficult. The hot summer sun was still high in the sky, but they had all had enough of seeing the sights for one day.

'There's another day tomorrow,' said Carl as he hoisted both little girls over his shoulders and carried them back to the car.

Matthew and Julie were waiting for them, sitting in the stuffy car with all the windows down. They looked happy enough, but were dying to get going so that they could put the air-conditioning on.

'Did you have a good day?' Jacky asked the young couple.

They both smiled and nodded. 'It was great!' Julie pronounced. 'But I'm longing for a shower.'

'We all are,' Carl remarked easily as he settled the girls on the back seat. 'And afterwards we can all meet in the hotel swimming pool.'

The Princesses squealed with delight, forgetting their tiredness. 'Can we come?' Charlotte asked.

'Of course; I did say all of us,' Carl assured her.

Within half an hour of arriving back at the hotel they were all in the swimming pool. Jacky had been careful to remove all traces of ointment from Helen's skin and was pleased to see that the eczema had reached a quiescent stage. The little girl's breathing had stabilised during the day, so there was absolutely no medical reason why she shouldn't take a swim.

Jacky stayed with her charged in the shallow end for a

while until Carl, looking bronzed and athletic, swam
over to help her out.

'Go and have a swim,' he ordered. 'I'll take care of
the girls. But don't get yourself too tired,' he added in a
gentler voice. 'Remember you have a date tonight.' He
trailed a finger lightly over her bare shoulder, and she
shivered as she swam away.

How could I possibly forget! she said to herself as she
swam out of reach of his tantalising fingers.

The sun was setting in a fiery glow beyond the tall oak
trees at the edge of the hotel grounds as Jacky closed the
windows of her room. No sound was to be heard from
the children's room next door, she noticed thankfully.
The Princesses had been exhausted after their long day
and had gone to bed uncomplaining. Julie and Matthew
had stationed themselves in the sitting area of the girls'
room for their stint of baby-sitting, with instructions to
ring down to the Oak Room Dining Room if they were
worried about anything. When she had left them, they
didn't seem to have a worry in the world, Jacky
reflected with a knowing smile. Yes, Carl was right
when he said there was a romance in the offing.

She glanced at her reflection in the long mirror by her
bathroom door. Is this skirt just a little too short? she
wondered anxiously as she surveyed the skimpy black
chiffon of the creation she had bought in Detroit. She
had been assured in the store that it was the very latest,
up-to-the-minute model, but now she was having her
doubts about it. It had seemed perfect when she tried
it on in the store with the assistant smiling her
approbation, but now . . .

Through her bathroom wall she heard the sound of
Carl singing happily as he splashed in his shower. Her
heart began to beat rapidly at the thought of the evening
ahead. It's only a simple dinner with the boss, she told
herself hurriedly, but the feeling of excitement and

apprehension wouldn't go away as she stepped into her high-heeled shoes. It was the first time she had spent so much money on herself, she reflected wickedly. Might as well enjoy myself!

The splashing had ceased and so had the singing. Jacky deduced that her escort must be dressing himself now. He's taking his time, she thought wryly. He doesn't seem in any hurry to start the evening. She flicked through a magazine as the minutes ticked by, and then at the sound of his knock on her door she had to hold herself back from racing to open it.

'Oh, Carl; how nice,' she said in a polite voice. Outwardly detached, she was tormented with nerves.

He took her arm and steered her towards the lift. The heady smell of his cologne drifted down to her and her tension mounted.

'Relax, girl!' he told her laughingly as the lift doors closed. 'You're all on edge.'

'Am I?' she asked ingenuously. 'I don't think so. I feel fine.'

She accepted his arm with alacrity as they walked along the thick pile of the corridor leading to the dining room. The feel of his strong body supporting her helped to calm her nerves, and by the time the waiter showed them to their table she was fully in control again.

'Mm, this is more like it!' she breathed as she looked around at the plush décor. The lights were so subdued that it was difficult to make out the exact details of the oak-panelled room, but there were candlelit areas where she could see couples dining amid the splendour of polished silver, sparkling white tablecloths and heavenly floral arrangements. The soft strains of Rachmaninov's Second Piano Concerto emanated from hidden speakers. It's so romantic! she thought as she smiled happily across at her escort.

'I'm glad you approve,' was his gentle response. 'I thought you needed taking out of yourself. You were beginning to look like a harassed housewife towards the end of this afternoon. But now—what a transformation! You look lovely, Jacky.'

'Thank you,' she replied quietly as she willed the start of a blush to vanish before Carl could see it.

The surgeon had ordered a couple of very dry Martinis and they sipped them peacefully as they soaked up the relaxing atmosphere. They had smoked trout with a Caesar salad of crisp romaine lettuce, bacon and croutons served with a spicy garlic dressing as a starter. This was followed by New York sirloin in a pepper sauce which the waiter told them was a speciality of the hotel.

'We'll pause for a while before our dessert,' Carl said with a smile. 'No point in rushing things. The night is young.'

Jacky smiled back at him, thinking how young and handsome he looked in the candlelight. He seemed to have shed all his worries for the evening, she reflected as she watched him pour her another glass of wine. She opened her mouth to remonstrate that she was feeling decidedly but happily hazy already, and then she had second thoughts. There was no point in trying to put a damper on their evening together. Who knew if there would ever be another? Carl was so unpredictable that she couldn't rely on his generosity again. She picked up her wineglass and looked across the table.

'I'm having a lovely evening, Carl,' she told him in a soft voice. 'You were right, we needed to get away by ourselves.'

He smiled and reached across the table to take her hand. 'I love to see you enjoying yourself, Jacky. You're the sort of girl who needs to be taken out and wined and dined. This . . . er . . . this friend of yours, the one you told me you were close to; was that Chris Douglas?'

Her heart began to thump so loudly that she felt

he must surely hear it. 'I didn't know him long before
. . . before he died,' she began hesitantly. 'Our
relationship didn't have time to flourish. He was fun to
be with—at first.' She hesitated and stared across at her
boss, wondering just how much she should unburden
herself. 'I was fond of him initially, but then he started
to become far too possessive. I knew I didn't want that
sort of relationship . . . with someone like Chris. I tried
to break it off on the day that . . .' she took a deep
breath to steady herself, 'on the day that he died. If only
he'd lived we might have had a chance to sort out our
relationship. He didn't deserve to die like that.'

'I'm sorry,' the surgeon stated quietly.

'Sorry?' Jacky repeated with ominous calm as she
snatched back her hand and laced her fingers tightly
together under the table. 'Being sorry won't bring him
back!' she flung at him in a throaty whisper.

'No, it won't,' he admitted evenly. A look of total
dejection had stolen over his face, removing all trace of
the boyish expression he had worn throughout the meal.
'Look, I don't feel hungry any more. Let's skip dessert
and go back to my room for coffee.'

He's evading the issue again, Jacky thought angrily.
But at last I've got him on the defensive. This is too
good an opportunity to miss! He wasn't going to escape
this time. She stood up quickly. 'Let's go,' she said
quietly as she made for the door.

The waiter looked surprised at their hasty departure,
but he produced the check for Carl's signature. The
surgeon came hurrying after Jacky and she revelled in
her feeling of power as she marched towards the lift. He
had actually confessed to being sorry, she remembered,
and a glow of satisfaction spread over her. Perhaps I'm
getting through to him at last!

Neither of them spoke until they were inside Carl's
room. Jacky looked around her, reflecting that it was
similar to her own, but with the added touches of Carl's

personal belongings it was very much a male domain. She perched on the edge of one of the armchairs while her boss rang down for coffee. There was an uneasy truce as they waited for room service. It was as if neither of them wanted to broach the subject that was uppermost in their minds for fear of being interrupted. When at last the young waiter had arrived and departed, leaving a pot of steaming coffee behind, Jacky drew a deep breath and fired the first shot.

'Well, at least you're sorry. I was beginning to think you were made of stone,' she observed icily.

'Quite the reverse. The whole experience of that young life being ended so abruptly has stayed with me night and day.' Carl ran his fingers through his black hair in a distracted movement.

'But how did it happen?' she asked heatedly.

'I don't know. He should never have been given that batch of insulin. I myself had reported that he was an unsuitable subject,' Carl replied in a deadpan voice.

'Why was he unsuitable?' she pursued eagerly.

'Because his diabetes was too mild to require such strong medication. His death was caused by an overdose of the new insulin product, but we had no idea who gave it to him.' The surgeon's face was grey with misery.

'But at the end of the day, you were in charge. You *should* have known!' Jacky declared firmly.

'Yes, I should,' he answered quietly. 'That's why I resigned.'

She stared at his dejected face and her heart went out to him. Maybe his usual devil-may-care demeanour was a sham to cover up what he knew, but she preferred it to his attitude of defeat, she thought. Perhaps he was simply trying to gain her sympathy. If that was the case then he's succeeded, she reflected wryly, as she reached out a hand to touch his cheek. 'I didn't realise you felt so strongly about it,' she said quietly. 'I'll try not to

quiz you any further, but Carl . . .' she stopped and
took deep breath. 'Please tell me if there are any new
developments. You see, Chris had no family. He was
adopted and his adoptive parents had died, so that he
had no one. That was why I felt it my duty—as his
friend—to find out what happened.'

Carl smiled and put a hand up to cover hers as it
rested lightly on his cheek. 'And you've been doing a
great job, Jacky,' he murmured. 'But leave it alone
now, there's a good girl. No good can come of poking
your nose in where it's not wanted. You might find
you've stirred up more than you bargained for. Trust
me . . .'

As he said these words he moved nearer to her and
put his lips against her forehead. 'I'd rather have you on
my side when it comes to the crunch,' he whispered.

Jacky turned to stare at him, puzzled by his cryptic
remarks, and their eyes met in a gaze of mutual trust.
Slowly his lips moved towards hers and she waited for
the feel of his tantalising mouth. His kiss was strong and
demanding as if it expressed a pent-up longing deep
inside him. Jacky responded with an urgency born of
relief and desire. As he took her in his arms she knew
she had never felt like this before. His skilful surgeon's
hands caressed her spine, and rivers of passion ran
down it. Her body felt as if it was made of molten metal
that was melting before a fiery furnace.

The knock on the door, when it came, brought them
both back to reality. Jacky stirred in Carl's arms and
stared up at him. How long had she been nestling here?
she wondered. Time seemed to have been standing still.
There was a bemused expression on the surgeon's face
as he relaxed his arms and stood up.

'No, don't move,' he told her gently as she began to
get up. 'I'll go.'

She ran a hand hastily through her tousled hair as she

heard Carl talking quietly at the door. And then she recognised Julie's voice. Heavens, it must be Helen's asthma! she thought, and immediately her sane professional self returned.

'I'm coming,' she announced as she leapt to her feet.

'We'll both go,' Carl told her firmly. 'But gather your wits together first, Sister.' He was smiling boyishly at her as he closed the door and returned to the sofa. 'You can't go looking like that!'

'I know.' She was feverishly rummaging in her bag for a comb and at the same time trying to avoid his scrutiny. She had no idea how she was going to be able to work with him after this romantic idyll, but she had got to pull herself together for the sake of their patient!

As soon as she entered the Princesses' bedroom Jacky could hear the typical wheezing sound of an asthmatic attack. Carl was close behind her and he went straight to Helen's bedside.

'She woke up suddenly, doctor,' Julie began to explain in a frightened voice. 'Then she sat up and started to cry because she couldn't breathe out properly.'

Carl nodded and knelt down beside the Princess's bed. 'Get the adrenalin 1:1000 solution, Sister,' he ordered brusquely. 'It's in my bag. I'll give her a hypodermic injection as an anti-spasmodic. Now Helen, it's all right dear. Just relax . . .'

The little girl clung to her favourite doctor, trying hard to do what he said. Jacky noticed the ominous cyanosis of Helen's face as she handed the syringe to her boss.

'Just a little prick,' the surgeon murmured to his patient as he skilfully injected the much-needed anti-spasmodic. Then he cradled the little girl soothingly in his arms as he instructed her how to breathe.

Within minutes the cyanosis had improved and Helen's normal high colour had returned. Jacky listened

to the gradual stabilisation of the breathing mechanism
and decided that the cure had been part medicinal and
part emotional. Once again she reflected that the great
Dr Harvey had a wonderful way of dispelling turmoil.
She watched him as he rocked the little Princess in his
arms, remembering the effect those strong arms had had
on her only minutes before . . .

'Helen's going to be OK now,' Carl pronounced after
about an hour of constant attention to the small patient.
'But I think Jacky should sleep in here tonight. Perhaps
you and Julie could change beds,' he suggested as he
regarded his Nursing Sister with a whimsical smile. 'You
would be able to detect changes in the breathing more
accurately than Julie.'

'Of course,' Jacky agreed quickly. She was only too
anxious to be near her patient, and also she wanted to
distance herself from Carl, With a whole room between
them there was no danger that she would overheard him
moving around. She wanted time to herself to think out
the new turn of events. It had all happened so quickly.
She had never meant . . .

'I'll leave Helen in your care, Sister.' Carl was being
deliberately professional and she was grateful for it.
'But don't hesitate to call me if you're worried,' he
added in a cool detached voice. 'Goodnight.' He
gathered up his things and made for the door without so
much as a backward glance.

Jacky busied herself with the clearing up and the
exchange of rooms with Julie. Helen had fallen into a
deep sleep of exhaustion and her respiration was
mercifully normal again. As Jacky turned out the light
she closed her eyes, willing herself to sleep. She was
tired out, but the excitement of the evening had stirred
up her emotions. Carl's face loomed in front of her
however hard she tried to think of something else. And
his words haunted her.

'You might find you've stirred up more than you

bargained for,' he had told her. What could he possibly mean?

CHAPTER EIGHT

FOUR THE next couple of days Jacky insisted that Helen should take things easy. Anything which might over-excite the little Princess was out of the question, she insisted. But on the final day of their stay in Niagara it was decided that they simply must go out on the *Maid of the Mist* boat. It had been one of the treats promised to the little Princesses, and Jacky agreed with Carl that it would be a terrible shame to miss it.

'Helen needs to get out now,' the surgeon observed as they were all taking breakfast together in the all-day restaurant. 'And so do you, Jacky,' he added, giving her a look which meant he wouldn't take no for an answer.

'I must admit it will be nice to leave the hotel again,' she said quickly. Two day's incarceration with the fractious little Princess had been extremely trying. Especially when the others had been enjoying themselves seeing the sights of Niagara! But she had been determined that her little patient would be totally fit before she ventured out into the big wide world again.

She met the surgeon's gaze with cool professional eyes as she thought that in many ways Princess Helen's demands on her time had been no bad thing. It had meant that she could spend long hours alone with her patient instead of going out and about with Carl. When he did call in to see them it was in a purely professional capacity, which was how she was anxious to keep their relationship. There had been time to consider the romantic evening they had spent together, and Jacky was anything but convinced about Carl's sincerity. He had told her to trust him, but why should she? Did he think he could overcome her doubts by his passionate embraces? she had tasked herself over and over again as she realised that she had allowed her heart to rule her head.

But her spirits lifted as they reached the river into which the mighty Niagara Falls were plunging. An early morning rainstorm was clearing and as the sun came out a huge rainbow spanned the valley.

'Can we look for the crock of gold?' Charlotte asked excitedly.

Carl smiled. 'I've been looking for it myself all my life and never found it,' he replied gently. 'I think you'll find that the end of the rainbow disappears as you approach it. So let's get on this boat,' he added quickly to console the little girl.

The princessess submitted to being encased in plastic raincoats again before they boarded the *Maid of the Mist*.

'Black ones this time,' Julie observed with a grin. 'They're not very flattering, are they, Matthew?'

'You look lovely, Julie,' he told her, and she felt happy to receive the compliment she had been fishing for. The last few days had been some of the happiest she had ever spent, she reflected contentedly. And all because of Matthew! She only hoped that he wouldn't change towards her when they got back to Detroit and she reverted to domestic drudge again.

They were filing across the narrow wooden gangplank and climbing into the boat. Carl carried Helen in his arms and Jacky followed behind holding Charlotte by the hand. Just for an instant she thought she saw the tall stranger whose appearance had given her the creeps in the lift under Niagara Falls. But no, I'm imagining things, she told herself quickly as the tall figure in front of Carl disappeared into the crowded boat. And there had been no way of seeing the colour of his hair, she reflected rationally. Everyone looks the same in these enormous long black raincoats. Carl was right: I do need a change of scene. My imagination is running riot!

The boat moved away from the landing stage carrying its heavy human cargo. Jacky leaned against the iron rail and pointed out the tiny figures of the tourists on the opposite bank of the river. Carl was holding Helen in his arms, in spite of her protests that she wanted to stand on the deck by herself. It was so crowded that the surgeon was afraid the little girl would have difficulty in breathing if she were down at child level.

The boat tossed wildly as they approached the gigantic Falls. It seemed as if they would capsize as the boat went within feet of the surging, splashing torrent.

'Now you see why we have to wear the raincoats,' Carl laughed, and Jacky smiled through the spray, hoping it wouldn't be long before the captain turned the boat round and headed for the safety of the riverbabnk. She glanced down into the boiling cauldron of water and knew that no one could possibly survive in such whirlpools.

Even as the thought occured to her she felt a change in the motion of the boat as it began to ease its way round in the other direction.

'Thank goodness!' she breathed, and Carl gave her a sympathetic smile.

'It's all plain sailing now,' he observed as the boat headed back towards the landing stage.

Jacky laughted as she noticed the relief on the faces of all the passengers. 'That was wonderful! But I was a bit scared,' she admitted to Carl.

'Don't worry. The captain does this several times a day, and he's never made a mistake yet. There's absolutely nothing that could go wrong with his navigation,' he remarked easily.

'I wonder where the lovebirds are?' Jacky said as she looked around at the other passengers.

'They're probably down belows holding hands and whispering sweet nothing,' he replied with a boyish grin. 'They probably haven't even noticed we've left the landing stage yet.'

Jacky laughed as she had a mental image of Julie and Matthew gazing into each other's eyes as the boat rocked on the turbulent water. 'Love does funny things to people . . .' she began, but her voice trailed away hastily as she saw the mellow look in Carl's eyes.

'Yes, doesn't it?' he replied, so softly that she wasn't sure if she'd heard him properly.

Jacky had no desire to continue the dangerous trend of the conversation and spent the remains of the journey back to the riverbank talking to Charlotte. There was a slight bump as the boat docked at the landing stage and then, all of a sudden, there was a great commotion from below decks.

'Man overboard!'

Jacky's blood ran cold as she heard the spine-chilling cry. She had often wondered if people actually said that when someone fell in. Well, now she knew . . .

'Here, take Helen.' Carl dumped the little girl uncermoniously into Jacky's arms. 'I'll go and see if I can help.'

She watched him forcing his way through the passengers as they clamoured to look over the side into the deep water.

'Disembark this way, please. Come along; keep moving!' called an offical voice as some of the crew tried to persuade the passengers to depart.

Jacky saw a young sailor diving into the water just as she noticed there were other figures swimming around there too.

'What happened? Did someone slip off the gangplank?' the woamn next to Jacky asked her.

'I've no idea,' Jacky volunteered. 'I wouldn't have thought so. It looks pretty safe to me . . .'

'Jacky where's Matthew?' Julie was making her agitated way through the passengers, her face white with fear. 'I can't find him.'

'Keep calm,' Jacky told the distraught girl, although she felt anything but calm herself. It couldn't possible be Matthew in the water, could it? she was asking herself. Maybe he's gone to see if he can help . . .

'One minute he was with me and the next he'd vanished!' Julie sobbed.

'Hush, you'll upset Helen,' Jacky whispered, and Julie made a valiant effort to control herself as she pressed against the iron rail to watch the rescue operation.

It was impossible to move either one way or the other, so the only useful thing to do was pacify the little Princesses, who were becoming impatient and agiatated.

'I want to get off this boat,' Charlotte declared in a peevish voice.

'So do I,' Helen wailed.

'It won't be long now,' Jacky soothed hopefully. 'Just as soon as . . . oh my God!' The exclamation came out involuntarily, but the next second she had regained her professional calm.

'It's Matthew! I can see his brown curly hair . . . It's Matthew,' sobbed Julie as an inert form was plucked from the water.

Jacky put Helen on the deck so that she could put her arm around the distraught girl. Looking down, she could see one of the sailors heaving Matthew on the concrete at the side of the river. The young man was still encased in his black plastic raincoat, but the hat had been lost in the water and there was no mistaking his face, grey though it was.

'Let this man through; he's a doctor,' she heard one of the sailors call out.

And then she saw Carl moving towards the prostrate

figure and gave a sigh of relief. If anyone can save him, Carl will, she thought as she watched the surgeon bending over his patient.

'What's he doing? Julie cried out

'Artificial respiration,' Jacky explained evenly. Don't let it be too late! she prayed as she watched for signs of life from the casualty.

The doctor worked on his patient with practised expertise, assessing that the young man had not been in the water very long. Within seconds his skill was rewarded as the victim's chest began to rise and fall rhythmically. Carl sat back on is heels, and breathed a sigh of relief as Matthew's eyes opened and he stared up at his boss.

'What happened?' The young man spluttered as he tried to speak.

'Take it easy, Matthew. We'll talk later. Just rest now,' Carl told him.

From somewhere at the top of the hill the sound of an amublance siren could be heard.

'I don't want to go to hospital,' Matthew whispered in a hoarse voice. He started to sit up, but his doctor restrained him gently.

'Just a formality,' Carl assured him. 'We'd better get a full check-up; have your chest X-rayed and so on. Then if you're OK I'll get you out. Believe me, I won't let them keep you in longer than necessary.'

The surgeon was as good as his word and managed to speed up all the procedures at the hospital. Matthew had made a remarkable recovery, and as soon as he was given the all clear, Carl was able to drive him back to the hotel.

Jacky was in the middle of putting the princesses to bed when she heard the welcome knock on their door. It had been a long tiring day trying to calm Julie and the little girls while Carl and Matthew were at the hospital, and the strain of waiting was beginning to tell on her. She hurried to the door and a delighted smile broke over her face as she saw her boss.

'Carl!' For a moment she forgot her resolution to be professional and flung her arms around his neck. Hastily, she tried to disentangle herself, but he was too quick for her. His hands had moved to hold her by the shoulders as he dropped a kiss on her forehead.

'What a welcome!' he drawled. 'I take it you're glad to see me.'

Jacky was immediately aware of the surprised stares of the girls behind her as she pulled herself away from Carl's embrace. 'How's Matthew?' she enquired in her professional voice.

'He's doing fine,' the surgeon told her. 'I've put him to bed in his room. They wanted to keep him in hospital for the night, but I said I could look after him here.' He strode into the room and was greeted with hugs from the two little princesses. 'Anyone would think I'd been away for a month instead of a few hours!' he smiled.

'We were so worried, sir,' Julie put in quickly. 'May I go and see Matthew now?'

Carl grinned amiably as he saw the young woman's deep concern etched into her worried face. Her usually well-kept fair hair looked as if she hadn't run a comb through it since early morning. 'Just for a little while—but not by yourself.' he added quickly as he saw the excitement mounting. 'I'll take you on there when I've checked on Helen and Charlotte. But you must be very quiet. Matthew needs rest and calm more than anything.'

'Have you discovered how it happened?' Jacky asked the question that was uppermost in all their minds.

'Matthew says he can't remember a thing,' the surgeon replied. 'He's still in shock, I think, so his memory of the incident will probably return. It would be unwise to question him at the moment. The main thing is that he's safe and well.'

'Will he be fit to travel back to Detroit tomorrow?' Julie asked anxiously.

'A good night's sleep will work wonders,' Carl reassured her. 'There'll be no need to change our plans if all goes well. I'll drive, of course, and Matthew can rest during the journey. He's a pretty resilent young man and his health was excellent before this little incident. He should recuperate rapidly . . . Now let me have a listen to Helen's chest.' He sat down on the little Princess's bed and fixed the end of his stethoscope in his ears. As his eyes met Jacky's at the end of the examination he nodded approvingly.

'Everything's fine here. Do you want to move back into your own room, Sister?' he asked over the top of the patient's head.

'I prefer to stay here,' Jacky replied hurriedly.

'Suit yourself,' the surgeon remarked in an impatient voice. He stood up and walked over to the door. 'Come along, Julie, let's go and see Matthew.'

Jacky watched the two of them disappear through the door. She was alone with her two little charges for her last night in Niagara. Perhaps I should have moved back to the room next to Carl's, she thought, and a tremor of disappointment ran through her. It was such an anticlimax . . .

'Read me a story, please,' clamoured Charlotte. 'The one about the baby whale who lost his mummy in the sea and . . .'

Jacky smiled as the little voice claimed her attention. One good thing about nursing was that you never had long to worry about yourself, she reflected happily.

The road back to Detroit seemed endless and boring as Jacky tried to amuse the little princesses. She glanced out of the window, thinking that the landscape had been practically the same for the past two hours. There were

long stretches of flat grassland punctuated by the
occasional cluster of houses, but nothing of any
significance. Carl had set the car on cruise control so
that the montony of the same speed was making her
sleep. But it was impossible to sleep with two fractious
children next to her. Julie, on the other hand, she
noticed, was dozing contentedly next to the window at
the other side of the children. I suppose she doesn't feel
the same sense of responsibility towards the girls as I do,
she thought, and gave a wistful sigh. It would be good
to get back to Detroit and hand over her charges to their
mother and the reliable Louise. The trip to Niagara
could hardly have been considered a holiday!

She looked at the back of Matthew's head as he
snoozed beside Carl. How dreadful it would have been
if he had drowned, she thought, and found herself
wondering how it could possibly have happened. Safety
arrangements on the boat had seemed excellent to her.
And Matthew was a grown man . . . There were so many
questions that she would have liked to ask the young
scientists about the dangerous escapades, but she knew
that Carol wouldn't allow his patient to be questioned
until he had fully recovered. She knew that Julie, too,
was even more mystified then she was, having been with
Matthew until just before the incident occured. But the
girl had agreed to respect the surgeon's ordered and had
refrained from questioning her friend.

The skyscrapers of Detroit had never looked so
inviting! Jackie thought as they crossed over the river
back into the United States. There had been no hold-ups
at the immigration checkpoint, she had been relieved to
find, and the little girls had become much more
amenable now that the end of the journey was in sight.

As the car pulled into the long driveway that led down
to the royal mansion, Jacky gave an audible sigh of
relief.

'I heard that!' laughed Carl, glancing in his rearview mirror. 'What's the matter, Sister? Didn't you enjoy the journey?'

'Not much,' she answered truthfully. 'It's been a great experience seeing Niagara Falls and all the other sights, but quite frankly, I'm ready to return to normal work.'

'Depends what you mean by normal work,' he smiled, and she saw the amusement in his eyes as she looked in the driving mirror.

'Well, I could do with a spell of off-duty,' she announced boldly, taking advantage of his good humour.

'Let's get back to the medical wing and assess the situation,' he volunteered in a careful voice. 'I'd love to give you a day off tomorrow. Heaven knows, you've earned it,' he added gently. 'But we'll have to see how things are going back at the ranch.'

Jacky smiled to herself at his facetiousness as the mansion came into view between the trees. Some ranch! she thought with a smile at the sight of the tall colonnades and marble pillars.

The security video system had alerted the royal parents of the approach of their offspring, and a smiling Prince and Princess emerged from the main building on to the wide stone step. There were hugs and kisses and even tears of joy as the royal family was united again.

'How are you feeling?', Jacky asked Princess Karine when some of the hubbub had died down.

'I'm fine,' the Princess replied easily. 'Never felt better.'

'We'd better examine you in the morning.' Carl put in hurriedly. 'Did you have to call in Dr Gregory?'

The Princess shook her head. 'No, I was a very good girl. Let's go inside.' She was anxiously staring around the grounds. Although the security system was efficient, she always had the feeling that someone might get

through and start taking pictures. And she knew that
her waistline had thickened considerably. It wouldn't be
long now before she had to make a conscious decision
whether to stay in her room until the confinement or
announce the news to the world. Her doctors would
prefer the latter, she knew that, but still she hesitated as
she remembered what she had suffered last time . . .

'How's your health?' Carl was asking the Prince as
they went inside the mansion.

Prince George assured him that the diabetes was fully
under control now.

'I'll give you a check-up tomorrow,' Carl told him as
he turned back to look at Matthew. In the commotion
of the welcome the young man had been forgotten.
'You'd better go to your room and rest. I'll be along
presently to take a look at you.'

'Isn't he well?' the Prince asked in a concerned voice.

'He had a little accident; got himself into difficulties
when he was out swimming,' Carl replied evenly.
'Nothing to worry about.'

What a master of understatement! Jacky thought
wryly. 'Do you mind if I go to my room now?' she
asked her boss.

'Please do,' he replied, and smiled down at her.
'Report for duty in the morning and when we've cleared
the clinic patients you can take the rest of the day off.
His eyes swept over her appraisingly. 'Sister has been a
tower of strength on our expedition. I couldn't have
coped without her,' he told the prince as Jacky walked
away.

'You're a lucky man,' Prince George said as the two
friends made their way to the royal apartments

A hot flush spread over Jacky's face as she pretended
not to hear the compliments. All she wanted at the
moment was some time to sort out her confused
thoughts.

The promised time off duty didn't materialise the

next day. It seemed as if the entire household had been waiting for their return to invade the morning clinic, Jacky thought ruefully as she said goodbye to the last patient. Most of the medical problems had been easy to deal with, but there had been the time-consuming examination of the Princess to contend with, not to mention the routine diabetic tests with the prince. Two hours had been set aside, during which, none of the other patients were allowed near the medical wing. Consequently, the morning clinic had now finished halfway through the hot afternoon.

'I'm sorry about your day off, Carl told her as they sipped the cold orange juice which Madeleine had just brought in for them.

'Can't be helped,' she observed. 'I had no idea there would be so much work involved in this assignment. At least when you're working in hospital you know when you're on and off duty, don't you?'

'But you don't regret coming out here, do you?' he asked gently.

'But you don't regret coming out here, do you?' he asked gently.

She could see the concern in his deep brown eyes as he leaned towards her across the desk and felt glad that there was an obstruction between them. It would be so easy to make a fool of herself again where Carl Harvey was concerned, she admitted wryly to herself. It was impossible to view the man rationally. Whenever they were alone her heart always took over from her head. 'No, I don't regret coming out here,' she replied carefully.

'We're a great team, you and I,' he continued eagerly. 'Come with me to Reichenstein, Jacky. It's a wonderful opportunity. You'd love it!' His eyes were shining with excitement at the prospect.

She took a deep breath as she tried to calm her thoughts. If only she could be sure that . . .

'I won't ask you again,' he put in quietly. 'I can see the prospect displeases you. Please forget I ever asked you.'

Jacky stared up into his solemn eyes and looked away hastily at the pain she read there. This wasn't simply a matter of her rejection of the plan, she told herself. There's another reason . . . something much more complicated. He's an extremely complicated man, she thought uneasily as she remembered her discussion with Matthew, the evening before. She had called in to see if the young man needed anything, and had been surprised to find that he seemed to recall the Niagara incident much better than Carl had indicated. He had told her that he had distinctly felt a sharp push from behind and then he had found himself in the water.

'I told Dr Harvey about this, but he told me I was rambling,' Matthew had confided to her.

And now, in the middle of this hot afternoon, she wondered what possible reason the surgeon could have for not reporting this . . .

'Have you checked on Matthew today, Carl?' she asked innocently.

'I looked in early this morning, but he was asleep,' the surgeon replied. 'I'll go and seen him as soon as we've finished here.'

'Does he remember anything about his dip in the river?' The query was made to seem deliberately light, but Jacky watched the surgeon's face with her full attention.

'He's still confused and it would be unwise to question him,' was the instantaneous reply.

Jacky stood up and busied herself with the final clearing up. Outwardly she seemed calm, but her thoughts were in turmoil. Carl had asked her to trust him, she remembered. But how could she when the mystery surrounding him was becoming more and more intense?

CHAPTER NINE

THE HOT summer wore on at the royal mansion, and Princess Karine found herself reluctant to stay inside. One day in early September she was sunning herself in a secluded part of the grounds when an over-zealous young reporter perched himself on the top of the high stone wall and took a photograph of her with the zoom lens. He was immediately chased away by a security man, but the picture appeared in the local press. There was immediate speculation about the Princess's bulky shape and, rather than deny the obvious, Her Royal Highness decided to come clean and announce her pregnancy. She was, after all, nearly seven months pregnant and there was every possibility that she would carry her baby to full term.

The local press were delighted with the scoop and the story was sold to all the national papers. Requests for television coverage were met with a firm refusal, but for several days reporters were allowed to interview the royal household, though strictly by appointment, and the interviews were carefully vetted. Carl and Jacky found themselves very much in demand, but confined their remarks to superficial observations about the pregnancy. They did not, for example, disclose any medical details. To the eyes of the world it seemed as if the Princess was undergoing a perfect pregnancy.

'And that's the way we must keep them thinking,' Carl told Jacky as they despatched the last reporter. From now on there were to be no more interviews until after the birth of the royal baby, and he was hoping that the press would not disregard his orders. He had insisted on extra security to patrol the grounds to ward off

unwanted intruders. 'The Princess must rest carefully
from now until her confinement. This is absolutely
essential.'

'Of course,' Jacky agreed quickly as she watched her
boss run his firm fingers distractedly through his thick
black hair. He's becoming more and more detached, she
found herself thinking as she noticed Carl's furrowed
brow. Whatever had happened to the devil-may-care
character who had wined and dined her at Niagara? she
wondered wistfully. Weeks had gone by in which he had
hardly spoken to her except to question her about a
patient. And the summer was drawing to its conclusion
and he was still refusing to take Jacky and the little
Princesses to Cape Cod.

Perhaps he's afraid of being alone with me again, she
mused. If that's the case, he's no need to worry, because
I've got myself under control again. She had told herself
again and again during the long hot summer that she
mustn't allow herself to become emotionally involved
with Carl. But every time he looked at her she had to
steel herself to be rational.

And he was looking at her now, she noticed as she
gathered together her things in preparation for going off
duty. It had been a long tiring day in which they had
found time to see the final reporter at the end of their
clinic patients. All Jacky wanted now was a cool
shower. But she would have to broach the subject of the
visit to Cape Cod. She had promised the little Princesses
she would. Every time she read their favourite story of
the baby whale and his mummy they clamoured to know
when the long-awaited expedition was to take place.
And Princess Karine too had quizzed Jacky about the
hold-up in the plans.

She met Carl's gaze without the flicker of an eyelid
and was encouraged by the warmth of those deep brown
pools. As nonchalantly as she possibly could, she began
her question. 'I was wondering when we could take the

Princesses to Cape Cod . . .?

'It's out of the question!'

His retort alarmed her. He had put her off before with vague words about his heavy schedule, but this was the first time he had categorically refused.

'But we promised!' she flung at him, her voice rising with indignation.

'Correction; *you* promised,' he countered angrily. 'I've never wanted to go down to Cape Cod. I haven't the time, for one thing. The recruitment for the Reichenstein project is still far from finished and . . .'

'But you can't disappoint Charlotte and Helen,' Jacky told him in a wheedling voice. This was her last resort, she thought grimly. If he wouldn't allow himself to be moved at the thought of the two little sad Princesses then nothing would change his mind. In that case she would have to make alternative arrangements. 'If you really can't make it I'm sure Matthew would take us,' she added quietly.

'No! I mean, he's too young to take on such responsibility.' Carl had carefully modified his tone after his initial negative response, but he looked thoroughly displeased at the suggestion.

'He's twenty-five; the same age as me.'

'But he's had no experience of royalty. And I need him to finish off a project he's working on in the laboratory.'

Ah, so that's the real reason, Jacky thought as she stood her ground, wondering what tack she should take next. Within seconds her boss had resolved the problem.

'If it means so much to Charlotte and Helen then we'll have to go,' he said quietly, and gave her a wry grin.

Her heart went out to him as she saw what the admission meant to him. She knew he hated defeat!

'Oh, thank you, Carl! The girls will be so happy. I'll go and tell Princess Karine now . . .'

'Steady on, Jacky!' He came round the desk and barred her way out of the door. 'We can't go until the end of this month. And we'd better fly down to Boston and hire a car from there—that means we'll only be away for a few days. I'll arrange the flight and the hotel. We don't need to take any of the staff with us. It will be much simpler to book for two adults and two children. We can play at Happy Families again.' He was smiling down at her now and some of his boyish charm had returned, she noticed as she grasped the doorknob. Now would be a good time to escape, she thought. Whenever Carl looked at her like that she found her resolve melting.

Outside in the corridor Jacky hurried away towards the royal apartments. It was a good time to catch the Princess in her sitting room. She's usually having tea at this hour, she thought as she tapped lightly on the Princess's door.

To her surprise, the Princess was not alone. It looked as if some kind of family conference was taking place as Louise ushered her into the sitting room.

'I can come back later, Your Highness,' Jacky began, when she saw that the Duchess and the Prince were also in the room.

Princess Karine raised her hand to quell the suggestion. 'Please stay and have some tea. You are most welcome. Bring another cup and saucer, Louise,' she ordered her maid. 'I was wanting to ask you about the Cape Cod holiday for the Princesses. Have any plans been made yet?'

Jacky smiled. 'This is what I came to see you about, ma'am.' She was always careful to observe the royal protocol when the Dowager Duchess was at hand; somehow Jacky felt that the old lady would disapprove if she were familiar with Princess Karine. She accepted a thin porcelain cup and saucer from Louise before launching into her report 'Dr Harvey is going to make the arrangements for the end of this month.'

'He's certainly taking his time,' Princess Karine remarked. 'I would have thought he would find a few days' relaxation at Cape Cod most agreeable after all his medical work here in Detroit. I get the distinct impression he doesn't want to go down there.'

'Well, of course he doesn't,' the Duchess observed quietly.

Jacky hadn't realised that the old lady had been taking any interest in the conversation, but now as she looked at her she realised that the Duchess was longing to express her opinion.

'What do you mean?' Princess Karine asked in a puzzled voice.

The Duchess ignored her and turned slowly to face her son. 'Isn't that where Victoria lives?' she asked in her wavering voice.

'Mother, it was all a long time ago. I think Carl has severed all contact with her . . .'

'Oh, the scandal when she left him!' his mother interrupted. 'My heart bled for him . . .'

'But he doesn't have to see her,' the Prince objected heatedly.

'Oh course he'll go to see her. I know him better than any of you,' the old lady replied sadly. 'He never got over it, you know. He still loves her.'

'Would somebody mind telling me what you're talking about?' the Princess asked softly.

'Oh, you didn't know about this?' The Duchess stared at her daughter-in-law in surprise. 'I'm not surprised; it was all hushed up. It wasn't entirely Victoria's fault, but . . .'

'Maman, *tais-toi, s'il te plaît!*' The Prince's command rang out over the sitting room, and after an initial scowl of displeasure the old lady became obediently silent. With quivering fingers she picked up her needlework and resumed her laborious petit-point.

'Have one of these little gateaux, Sister Diamond,'
Princess Karine suggested sweetly as she tried to ease the
tense atmosphere.

'Thank you.' Jacky accepted one of the small sugary
cakes, but she left it sitting on her plate. Somehow she
found she had no appetite as she contemplated the
startling revelation. Who was this mysterious Victoria
who had left Carl? she wondered miserably. No wonder
he didn't want to go down to Cape Cod. Especially if he
still loved her . . .'

She excused herself as soon as she could and made her
way back to her room. Princess Karine had indicated
that they would get together at a later date to finalise the
arrangements, and Jacky had been quick to agree. The
atmosphere in the Princess's sitting room had not been
conducive to decision-making.

In the days that followed there were many occasions
when Jacky would have liked to make enquiries about
the unknown Victoria, but she remained silent. If there
was some awful scandal it was far better that she didn't
know about it, she reasoned. And if Carl wanted to go
and see the woman he still loved while they were at Cape
Cod then that was his affair.

As the throbbing jet soared into the late September sky,
Jacky breathed a sigh of relief. 'We made it!' she
smiled, gazing out at the white flecks of clouds beneath
them.

'Was there ever any doubt about it?' Carl asked with
a whimsical smile.

She turned away from the window and gave him a
withering look. 'Dr Harvey,' she began in a pseudo-
professional voice, 'how you can sit there and say such a
thing when you know you blocked all my initial
attempts to get this expedition moving——!'

'I know; I wasn't at all keen . . .'

'What an understatement!' she countered, but her tone was light and bantering. There was no point in dispelling his newfound mood of optimism. It was far preferable to the dejected man she had got used to of late.

'Now that we're actually off the ground I think it's a good idea to be going to Cape Cod,' Carl admitted gently.

'So do I!' cried little Helen as she squirmed to get a more comfortable place on Jacky's knee. 'We're going to see Jimbo the Whale and his mummy.'

'Well, I hope we're going to see him,' Jacky put in quickly. 'If we go out in a party of whale-watchers we should be able to see him—or one of his friends . . .'

'We shall see Jimbo!' Helen reiterated as she gave Jacky a hug.

'I do hope she won't be disappointed,' Jacky whispered to Carl as the little Princess was staring out of the window.

'The whale-watching boats are fairly reliable,' he replied quietly. 'If there's a whale in the vicinity the captain will find it. And then it will be so exciting for them to watch. I'm going to take some photos.'

'I take it you've been on one of these expeditions before, have you?' Jacky asked evenly.

'Oh yes; only once,' he told her. 'But it's not to be missed, I can tell you.'

'Then why did you fight me over our little trip?' she queried.

He put a long tapering finger under her chin and looked into her eyes. 'You ask too many questions, my girl. One of these days you'll wish you weren't so inquisitive.'

She smiled at him calmly, but her heart was beating quickly. 'I have an enquiring mind,' she told him blandly.

'You've said it?' he retorted as he turned away to give

his attention to Charlotte.

A hire car was waiting for them at the airport and they covered the final lap of their journey in the late afternoon. The sun was dipping down into the sea at Provincetown on the very end of Cape Cod as they pulled up in front of their hotel. The Princesses had been asleep for the last hour and had therefore missed the spectacular scenery as Carl drove down the length of Cape Cod. Jacky had been thrilled to catch glimpses of the sea on either side of their thin strip of land, and she was now enthralled with the beautiful sunset view.

Carl had ordered a suite of rooms in the hotel, and Jacky was most impressed as she flung wide the long windows of the sitting room and walked out on to the balcony.

'Rather pricey, isn't it?' she remarked as Carl joined her, standing behind her and breathing in the tangy air of the sea with obvious enjoyment.

'Mm, the air's good out here after being cooped up all day,' he enthused. 'Don't worry about the cost. Princess Karine insisted I order the best rooms for her daughters, and from a security point of view, it's best if we're all in the same suite . . . Just look at that fabulous moon!'

Jacky was already gazing at the fiery ball in the dark velvet sky. Tiny diamonds punctuated the impressive backcloth and further lit the natural scenery surrounding the mysterious ocean. In the nocturnal light she could make out the shapes of several tall ships anchored near the shore and on the furthest point of land the reassuring beacon of the lighthouse shone out in a welcome glow. The sheer beauty of the scene made her sigh with pleasure and she could feel herself relaxing all the tensions of the long tiring day.

Carl's hand on her shoulder made her tense up automatically. He was standing so close behind her that she could imagine his heart beating. He had changed into a thin cashmere sweater and she could feel the smooth texture against her bare shoulders. They had put the children to bed and Jacky knew that now the time was their own for a few hours.

'I've ordered room service,' he told her gently. 'It will be safer not to leave the children alone.'

She drew in her breath sharply. The setting was so romantic—a luxury suite overlooking the ocean, the children safely tucked up in bed. What did Carl have in mind? she wondered as she turned tentatively to face him.

He put both hands on her shoulders and looked down enquiringly into her eyes as he said,

'I have to go out, Jacky. There's someone I must see.'

She stared back aty him and hated herself for the feeling of disappointment that flooded through her. Yes, she had been so looking forward to an evening with Carl, she realised. She had told herself that the Prince had been right when he predicted that Carl wouldn't necessarily have to see the mysterious Victoria; that even if he still loved the woman, as the Duchess had indicated, he wouldn't want to open up old wounds. But obviously he felt the old attraction was too much for him.

'Do you have friends in the area?' she asked lightly.

He smiled and put a finger under her chin. 'Questions, always questions! Keeρ the door to your room locked and don't admit anyone while I'ɱ away except room service. I won't be late.'

He was still smiling as he turned on his heel and headed for the door. Jacky watched him go with a sinking feeling. He had a perfect right to go wherever he pleased, she reminded herself rationally. And he had discharged his duty as a doctor by giving Helen an extensive chest examination this evening. So he was under no obligation to stay in and spend the evening with Jacky. After all, she thought, I haven't exactly given him any encouragement since our last romantic evening together in Niagara. Quite the reverse! He probably thinks I still dislike him intensely . . .

A tap at the door interrupted her wistful thoughts and she went to admit the room service waiter. She found that Carl had ordered supper for one, so he had obviously intended to dine out this evening. Maybe Victoria's a good cook, she thought enviously as she removed the lids from the dishes that the waiter had spread out on the white tablecloth.

She ate her lonely supper of Cape Cod scallops which had been deep fried to a golden brown and garnished with a crisp green salad. They were delicious, but her appetite seemed to have vanished. After a feeble attempt she pushed the food away and decided to have an early night. She went into the girls' bedroom and listened to Helen's breathing. When she had satisfied herself that all was well she retired to her own room and sank down on to the huge king-size bed. She found herself wondering if he would return that night or if he would succeed in a reconciliation with his erstwhile beloved and not return until morning. Maybe that was why he had made such a thorough check on Helen. The Duchess had said that when Victoria left Carl there had been a scandal, she remembered. Then that could only mean that they had been married . . .

Jacky jumped off the bed and went into her bathroom before she could depress herself further. As she lowered herself into the bath she tried to convince herself that it was none of her business.

Later, as she lay in bed trying to sleep, she found that her ears were constantly tuned to the sound of Carl's key in the door. When it came she sat bolt upright and switched on the light. Better make sure it's Carl and not an intruder, she thought anxiously as the heard stealthy footsteps crossing the sitting room.

'Carl?' she called hesitantly.

The footsteps hurried to her door and she watched as the handle moved downwards.

'Not asleep yet?' Carl stood in the doorway smiling in at her.

'I was afraid to sleep until you came in,' she told him quickly.

He moved into the room and her heart started to thump madly. 'Well, now I'm here, so all's well. I looked in on Helen and Charlotte. They were sleeping peacefully.'

He had reached the side of her bed and she was suddenly aware of her revealing nightgown. It was her one and only item of sheer luxurious lingerie and had been wildly expensive in Detroit. It made her feel like a million dollars when she wore it, but she hoped Carl didn't think she was wearing it for his benefit, because she wasn't! she told herself convincingly as she stared at his smug self-satisfied expression. He certainly looked as if the evening had been a success!

He sat down on the side of her bed and she moved away from him.

He laughed at her discomfort. 'Don't be such a prude, Jacky! I've seen lots of nightdresses before, but this must surely be the prettiest.' He reached out to touch the slender white lace strap on her shoulder. 'Mm, I like that.'

As he bent his head to kiss the spot where his fingers had lingered she recoiled as if he was going to strike her.

'No, don't' she cried out in an anguished voice. 'I don't want you to touch me. We both know that we can't go on like this.'

'Like what?' queried Carl with ominous calm as he pulled himself away from her.

'Pretending that everything's all right between us when all the time we know that there's no future in it,' Jacky flung at him heatedly.

'What's the future got to do with it? I was thinking

about the present. And at this particular moment, Jacky, you look so desirable . . .' he began, but she covered her ears.

'Stop it! I don't want to snatch a secret moment here, a furtive moment there,' she told him angrily.

'What do you want?' he asked gently, and made as if to move back on to her bedside.

'I want you to get out of my room!'

Seconds of silence elapsed after her heated words while she stared at him, her eyes blazing with fury. And then all her pent-up frustration broke loose and she began to cry. Carl's arms went around her shaking shoulders as the anguished sobs were wrenched from her.

'Please go away,' she told him as his strong arms pulled her towards him. 'Why must you torment me like this?'

'I'm sorry,' he said quietly as he relinquished his grasp. 'I didn't mean to upset you. Forgive me.'

He was stading up as he said this, and through her tears Jacky thought that he had never looked so handsome and dignified. For an instant she wondered if his wife had found him as attractive as she had. Perhaps they had made love and that was why he had come in looking so pleased with himself. And perhaps he had planned that she should be his second conquest of the evening. . .

But he was leaving her now, and she hurriedly dried her tears. As he turned at the door he smiled sadly. 'Get a good night's sleep. We've another long day tomorrow,' he told her brusquely as he quietly closed the door.

Jacky heard him moving around in his room and found it impossible to sleep until all was still again. As she put out the light she heard Carl's voice speaking softly. It was obvious he was on the phone, as she could hear no other voice replying to him. She was sorely

tempted to pick up the phone and listen in, but she
couldn't bring herself to be so underhand. He's entitled
to his own private life, she told herself. And anyway, I
don't want to know, was her final thought as she buried
her head in the pillow.

CHAPTER TEN

THE SUN was blazing down out of a cloudless sky as Jacky pulled back the curtains of her room. She could hear the little girls playing in their room next to hers and on the other side of her there was the noise of splashing in the shower, accompanied by vague sounds of singing. Carl seems pleased with himself today, she thought, and deliberately pushed all thoughts of the night before from her mind.

Her only concern now was for her little charges. She must make sure that they had the best attention during these last days of her assignment in America. The royal family would be flying back to Reichenstein soon after they got back from Cape Cod and her services would no longer be required. Carl would accompany them back to their country to set up his medical project there, but Jacky had no intention of taking up the offer of a job. All she wanted to do was end this assignment and forget that Dr Carl Harvey had ever existed.

As for the inquiry into the death of Chris Douglas, she had decided to let that take its own course. She would presumably read about it in the press when it was eventually concluded, but she was not going to become further involved. The fact that the case had not been closed had been a pleasing revelation to her. And she was also heartened by the fact that she had learned that Chris had been given the drug by mistake but that steps had been taken to ensure that this could not happen again. That's some consolation, she thought as she went along to take care of the little Princesses. If Carl is hiding the facts from me he probably has a good reason. But the inquiry is sure to catch up with him, she thought

147

sadly as she put on a professional smile for her charges.

It was difficult to contain the girls' excitement at the prospect of a day on the water.

'We're goint to see Jimbo!' Charlotte chanted continually as they walked along the esplanade leading to the whale-watch boats.

Jacky was surprised to find that there were several boats prepared to take them out to view the whales. The choice of which one was left to the Princesses, who had never been on a public boat before. Naturally, they chose the one with the brightest colours and loudest music, and they ran happily up the gangplank and on to the top deck. The music ceased as the ship set sail, presumably so as not to scare away the whales.

They sailed along the final curve of the Cape Cod coastline, beyond the last vestige of sandy dune and out towards the ocean.

'We must have come a long way,' Jacky remarked to Carl after about an hour.

'The whales are a long way from shore,' he explained, keeping his eyes focused on the horizon. 'But the captain knows how to find them. You're not cold, are you?' he asked in a concerned voice.

She shook her head. Although the sun was beating down there was a fresh breeze which became cooler as they progressed out to sea. Little Helen had snuggled against her for warmth, but the Princess was well wrapped up against the wind. Charlotte sat on the other side of Jacky staring out to sea, intent on being the first person to shout, 'There she blows!'

'Do they really shout that when they see the whale?' the elder Princess asked her nurse solemnly.

'You'll soon find out,' Jacky told her as the messages about the whales' whereabouts became more frequent over the ship's tannoy system.

'Over there!' someone called suddenly, and the entire cargo of passengers ran to the side of the ship so that

Jacky felt the list towards the water and was afraid the
ship would capsize on that side. Excitedly the passengers
scoured the sea with their eyes. All manner of
photographic equipement was produced as they waited
for the big moment.

Jacky was clinging tightly to Helen while Carl held on
to Charlotte, who seemed determined to reach into the
water as the ship dipped towards it. But it was a false
alarm, the captain explained over the tannoy, and there
were groans of disappointment.

But even as the passengers groaned a huge whale
loomed up out of the water only yards from the ship.

'It's Jimbo!' cried Charlotte as she tried to climb up
the side of the ship.

Carl laughed as he held on to the little girl, and the
entire cargo of passengers broke out into cries of delight
and excitement.

The huge creature reared itself out of the water and
turned a doleful eye on the noisy spectators.

'It must be forty feet long!' Jacky remarked, unable
to believe her own eyes as she watched the monster. And
then she noticed that a smaller whale had come to the
surface. The baby whale was perhaps about twenty feet
long, and it was keeping close to its mother and trying to
copy her spectacular movements.

'That little one is Jimbo and the big one is his
mummy,' Helen announced quietly. She was holding on
to Jacky as if her life depended on it. The excitement of
seeing the long-awaited mammals had made her short of
breath and she was beginning to wheeze.

Jacky produced an inhaler from her bag and put it to
the little girl's nostrils. 'We'd better go below,' she told
her small patient, but the little girl protested at the idea.

'Not until Jimbo's gone away,' she insisted.

Carl looked across at Jacky. 'Let her stay here until
the whales have disappeared,' he said with a wry smile
as he held out his arms to take charge of their patient.

Helen curled up against the surgeon's chest, but kept her eyes still on the cavorting pair in the sea as she struggled to catch her breath.

It was almost as if the whales knew they were giving a public performance, Jacky thought as she saw the way they leapt up out of the water and came down in a wide curve, their tails wiggling above the surface before they disappeared from view.

As the ruffled sea became smooth again, Carl took his little party below into the warmth of the cabin. He spoke soothingly all the time to the small patient in his arms, and after a few minutes her breathing returned to normal and the bluish tinge around her nostrils disappeared.

Jacky felt the movement of the ship as it changed course and headed for home. 'Here, let me take Helen,' she said to her boss, who had been nursing the child since the beginning of her asthmatic attack. She reached out and took the now somnolent child from his arms.

'I'll get us some coffee.' He stood up and eased his long cramped legs.

Jacky watched him walking over to the little bar, and felt something akin to despair at the thought that soon he was going to walk out of her life for ever. She turned away from the little Princesses so that they couldn't see the tear that had risen unbidden in her eye. If only . . . she thought wistfully as she stared out of the porthole at the grey waves. If only things were different . . .

A strong wind had blown up and the ship began to rock from side to side, clattering the bottles of Coca-Cola and fizzy lemonade on to the floor. The waves were now topped with white caps of blown spray and the sky was covered over with dark ominous clouds. As the first drops of rain pounded heavily on the deck above Jacky shivered and the little Princesses snuggled even closer to her. Carl's arm was resting lightly on the back of her seat, but it was purely a protective gesture.

She knew he wouldn't try to stir up their emotional relationship again. It was over, even before it had begun, she told herself firmly.

As they pulled into port Carl turned to Jacky and smiled. 'Did you enjoy that?' he asked in a bright impersonal voice.

'I wouldn't have missed it for anything,' she replied truthfully.

The little girls stirred and opened their eyes at the sound of their voices. They had slept for most of the rough journey home and were now full of life again.

'What are we going to do now?' Charlotte asked happily.

'We'll go and look round the town,' Carl replied as he took the little Princesses by the hand and began to negotiate their way off the ship. 'It's a fascinating place.'

Jacky was relieved to see that the rain had stopped and the sun was peeping out from behind a cloud as they stepped ashore. Carl guided them through a maze of narrow streets, pointing out buildings of interest until he stopped in front of the museum.

'I have to leave you here for a while,' he said quietly, deliberately avoiding Jacky's searching eyes. 'Go inside and I'll join you in a little while. There's a replica of a Provincetown kitchen at the turn of the century which the girls will love to see. It has lifelike figures of a mother and child and perfect imitations of cookies and pies . . .'

'Oh yes, let's go in there!' cried Charlotte, pulling on Jacky's hand.

'How long will you be?' Jacky asked her boss in an even tone.

'Not long . . . I have to see someone for a few minutes . . .' he faltered uneasily.

Jacky turned away and ushered her charges up the museum path. 'Take all the time you want,' she remarked evenly. 'We'll see you back at the hotel.'

If Carl made any reply to this remark Jacky would not have heard it as she hurried inside the cool interior. The girls were chattering excitedly as she purchased tickets. Let him spend the rest of the day with Victoria! she thought indignantly. He needn't think he's indispensable. We can get along perfectly well without him!

'Which way is the pretty kitchen?' Charlotte asked the woman on the door.

'Through there, dear,' the woman replied with a smile as she pointed out the direction.

Jacky hurried after her exuberant charges. When they had spent a few minutes admiring the lifelike replicas they moved on to look at a beautiful antique fire engine. As she turned away her eyes caught sight of a spectacular watercolour hanging on the wall behind them. The broad sweeping colours of the seascape intrigued her as she stepped up to take a closer look. The artist had captured the mood of the angry ocean perfectly, Jacky thought as she remembered the white-capped waves she had seen only a couple of hours ago.

'Storm on the Horizon', the picture was called. She read out the title and leaned closer to decipher the artist's name. 'Victoria Harvey,' she read, and the name blurred before her eyes as her pulses began to race. In a small town like this could this possibly be Carl's wife?

The helpful lady on the door was watching her reaction and called out,' Do you like that one? Mrs Harvey is one of our favourite artists in Provincetown.'

'It's very beautiful,' Jacky heard herself saying as she gazed at the wide canvas. 'Is it for sale?'

'Well now, that I couldn't say. We borrowed it for our exhibition, you see. You'd have to go and ask Mrs Harvey . . . She only lives round the corner. Turn left as you go out the door and it's the white house, set back from the road.'

'Thank you. Come along, girls,' Jacky said firmly.

She had no idea what she was going to do, but she just had to solve the mystery of Victoria Harvey. And if it meant buying a picture, well, so be it, she thought. Anyway, it would be a wonderful souvenir of her American assignment; something she would always treasure.

She hurried along the narrow pavement clutching tightly to the girls' hands. As they rounded the first corner she saw the white house which had been described to her. It looked delightfully feminine with its pretty pink curtains and roses climbing round the door. Even as the thought occurred to her the door opened and a familiar figure emerged. She held her breath as she saw him turn to embrace someone inside. It was impossible to see clearly what the woman was like, but Jacky caught a glimpse of a slim figure in blue jeans and a cream sweater.

And her hair was definitely blonde, she remembered, as she watched the door closing. Suddenly all desire to investigate further had left her. Up till now she had hoped that there might have been some mistake, that she was torturing herself unnecessarily. But no; now that she had seen Victoria Harvey in the flesh . . .

'Dr Harvey!' Charlotte cried as she recognised the tall figure walking down the path towards them.

He stopped for an instant and then quickened his step. 'What on earth are you doing here?' he asked as he reached them.

'Sister was going to buy a painting from a lady who lives along here,' Charlotte replied eagerly, unaware of the tension she was creating.

Carl stared down at her. 'Would you like an introduction?' he asked evenly. 'Or were you merely spying on me?' he whispered harshly in Jacky's ear.

'I've changed my mind about the painting, girls,' Jacky announced brightly. 'Let's go back to the hotel.'

Carl reached for her arm and steered her back along the street, his faced a mask of cold contempt. Happily the little girls were unaware of the hostility between the doctor and nurse as they were shepherded back to their hotel. Jacky's head was throbbing with remorse. How could she have been so insensitive! she asked herself. How many times had she reminded herself that Carl's life was his own affair?

They had an early supper in the large impersonal hotel dining room. No more candlelit dinners à deux! Jacky thought reluctantly as she helped Helen to cut up her chicken and chips. Looking around the room, she realised that they looked like an average family on holiday; mum, dad, two kids . . .

'Are you staying in tonight?' she asked Carl in a quiet voice. They had spoken only the bare essentials of conversation since leaving the town centre.

'Yes; I have some paperwork to catch up on,' he replied brusquely.

How exciting! Jacky thought sarcastically. 'I shall have an early night,' she told him evenly.

He nodded and then continued to ignore her as he turned his full attention on his little charges. As soon as the meal was finished they all went back to the suite and began preparations for the girls' bedtime. Carl did a chest examination on Helen and pronounced her fully recovered from the asthma attack earlier in the day. He then excused himself, saying he had work to do, and left Jacky to bathe and put the girls to bed. As soon as she had finished she went into her own room and locked the door. She wanted no interruptions tonight! she told herself firmly.

She was awakened early in the morning by the sound of the telephone ringing, but before she could reach out her hand it stopped. From next door came the sound of Carl's subdued voice. Jacky looked at the phone but had no desire to pick it up and listen in. Let him have his early-morning call in peace! she thought, and closed her eyes to try and go back to sleep. Seconds later there was a knocking on her door.

'Jacky, let me in!' The surgeon sounded upset about something.

'Just a minute,' she told him as she searched for her robe.

'We have to go back to Detroit,' he told her in a breathless voice as she opened the door.

'Why?' she asked in alarm, and held the door wide open so that he could come inside.

'Madeleine just rang. Princess Karine had abdominal pains in the night—they may be uterine contractions. I've instructed her to get in touch with Jim Gregory . . .'

'Shouldn't she be admitted to hospital?' Jacky asked quickly.

'Of course she should,' he snapped. 'But Princess Karine is the most stubborn patient I've ever encountered, and she refuses to budge until I arrive back. I hoped Jim might talk some sense into her . . . But we've got to get a move on. Get the girls up while I phone the airport.'

Jacky was clinging tightly to Helen as she ran up the steps of the royal mansion. The mad dash back to Detroit had been a great strain on the little asthmatic, but with the calming effect of her doctor and Sister she had managed to stave off an impending bout of dyspnoea. Charlotte had behaved impeccably throughout, having been told of her mother's indisposition. The seriousness of the complication had been played down, but even so the elder of the two Princesses was looking worried.

'You will take care of Mummy, won't you, Dr Harvey?' she begged as they went inside the house.

'I'll do everything I can . . . Where is the princess?'

Carl asked a harassed-looking Louise who was waiting in the entrance hall.

'*Paqr ici, monsieur le docteur.*' The maid hurriedly indicated the medical wing before taking charge of the little Princesses with a brusque, '*Venez, mes enfants.*'

Carl and Jacky made their way quickly towards the medical wing. Madeleine was holding back the swing doors in readiness for their arrival.

'Dr Gregory is with the Princess,' she informed them evenly.

'Thank God for that!' said Carl under his breath as he crossed to the examination room.

Jacky moved in behind him, and was immediately shocked to see the worried look on Jim Gregory's face. The obstetrician pulled them on one side so that the Princess could not hear what he had to say.

'We've got to persuade her to be admitted to hospital,' he whispered urgently. 'She's going into premature labour.'

'Have you removed the Shirodkar suture?' Carl asked quickly.

'Not yet; but it will have to come out soon. She's thirty-two weeks pregnant and the foetal heartbeat is excellent. The baby will be born alive if we act quickly. But it's going to need special care, and we haven't the facilities here . . .'

A loud wailing took them all flying to the Princess's bedside. 'Help me—I can't bear it! Oh, Carl, thank goodness you're here!' The Princess held out her arms to clutch at her favourite doctor.

For several seconds the surgeon allowed himself to comfort the Princess before he gently eased away her hands so that he could examine the birth canal for himself. His face was grim as he turned to his colleague.

'Remove the suture,' he ordered quietly. 'We can't take chances with the baby's life.'

The obstetrician nodded in agreement and turned to

Jacky. She had already prepared the instruments he would require and handed them to him wordlessly before stepping back to watch the intricate procedure. As Dr Gregory eased away the Shirodkar suture the cervix dilated, and Carl leaned forward to examine it.

'Delivery is imminent,' he whispered to Jacky. 'Swab the vulval and perineal areas.'

Jacky reached for the bottle of Hibitane 1 in 1000 and carried out his instructions before spreading sterile towels on the surrounding areas. Carl was hurriedly explaining to Princess Karine that all would be well if she pushed when he instructed and refrained in between contractions. The patient was groaning miserably and clinging to her doctor's hand.

'I'll take over here,' said Jacky as she moved up the bed to take the patient's hand in her own. With the other hand she wiped the Princess's damp forehead. Carl flashed her a gateful smile as he returned to the foot of the bed to help his colleague with the delivery.

'We've got the head,' he announced at the end of a particularly strong contraction.

Princess Karine lay back on the pillow, panting breathlessly. 'I hope it's a boy,' she whispered.

Jacky smiled. 'Can't tell at this stage,' she told her patient sympathetically. 'You're doing fine; won't be long now.' She picked up a cool sponge and wiped the sweat off the weary Princess's face.

Carl was holding the baby's head and feeling to make sure that the umbilical cord was not round its neck. As the next contraction came the shoulders and body were expelled and the surgeon delivered the baby in an upward direction, following the physiological curve, and placed it straight on the Princess's abdomen.

'It's a boy!' he announced, and there was no mistaking his feeling of triumph at the successful outcome.

The tiny Prince gave a weak cry at being brought out

into the strange world of bright lights and grasping
hands.

'Let me hold him,' the Princess cried as Jacky hastily
wrapped the infant in a sterile cloth. 'Oh, he's so
tiny!'

Jacky watched the delighted mother gazing down at
her newborn child and her eyes caught sight of Carl's
obvious relief. Surgeon and Sister smiled at each other
in mutual satisfaction.

'Ring the Detroit Medical Center, Sister.' Carl's voice
was husky with emotion. 'The number's on my desk.
Tell them we want an ambulance with an incubator. Our
little Prince is going to need some help with respiration.'
As he said this, the surgeon leaned forward to remove
the infant from his mother's arms so that he could cut
the cord.

Jacky pulled her mask down and hurried out of the
room. The door to Carl's office was slightly open and
she was about to go inside when she heard Madeleine
calling her from across the corridor.

'Sister Diamond!'

Jacky turned at the sound of the secretary's voice.
'My, we are being formal . . .' she began, but one look
at Madeleine's ashen face made her pause and take a
step towards her. 'What's the matter, Madeleine?' she
asked gently. On closer inspection she could see the
drawn lines of anxiety under the thick make-up.
I've never seen her looking so old, she thought in
surprise.

'I have to go away,' was the brief explanation. 'Give
this to Dr Harvey.'

Jacky took the white envelope and stared in
amazement at the secretary. 'Wouldn't it be better if
you gave it to him yourself?' she asked quietly.

'No! No, I can't face him . . . It's better this way.'
Madeleina had moved out of her office and Jacky saw
that she was already carrying a suitcase.

Jacky put the letter in her pocket. 'It's obvious I can't dissuade you,' she remarked reluctantly. 'And I have to get on now.'

But Madeleine was disappearing through the swing doors before Jacky had finished speaking. She had no time to worry about the secretary as she turned back towards Carl's office. She wondered, fleetingly, if Madeleine had discovered about Carl's reunion with his wife. After all, she had been his personal secretary and close companion for a long time. It was inevitable she would know about Victoria . . .

Putting the thought deliberately out of her mind, Jacky pushed open the surgeon's door—and stopped in amazement at the sight which confronted her. Matthew was leaning over the filing cabinet desperately searching through one of the drawers. His back was towards the door, but he turned at the sound of her footsteps, clutching a sheaf of papers in his hand.

'I wasn't aware that your scientific research necessitated delving into Dr Harvey' private filing cabinet,' Jacky said evenly.'

Still clutching the papers, the young man made as if to move round the desk, but the sound of the surgeon's firm tread in the corridor caused him to stop in his tracks.

'Have you made that phone call . . .?' Carl began, then stared across the room at his assistant. 'What exactly do you think you're doing, Matthew?' he asked in an ominous tone.

'I can explain, sir,' Matthew replied desperately. 'You've got to listen to me . . .'

'I will listen, but I don't think we need involve Sister Diamond.' Carl turned to face Jacky and she thought she had never seen him looking so angry. 'Go back to our patient and help Dr Gregory,' he instructed her with quiet calm. 'I'll deal with this.'

'But I haven't rung the hospital yet.'

'Good God, woman, what the hell have you been doing?' Carl strode over to the desk and picked up the phone. 'I'll do it myself . . . No, stay where you are, Matthew! I need an explanation.'

Jacky beat a hasty retreat and closed the door on the unpleasant confrontation. It was a relief to get back into the labour room and witness the joy that the new arrival had provoked. Prince George was leaning over his wife in wonderment and murmuring over and over again, 'A son, a son!' as is he couldn't believe his good fortune.

Several minutes later Carl returned. His face was grim, but he made no allusion to the distressing incident. Jacky had no time to wonder at the outcome as she busied herself with the post-natal care of the tiny infant. She was relieved when she was able to place him in the incubator which arrived with the ambulance.

As the ambulance raced through the streets of Detroit towards the Medical Center, Jacky kept a firm watch on her tiny patient. The infanty's colour had improved with the administration of oxygen, but she could see that the premature lungs were having difficulty with respiration. She turned to look at Carl, who was tending the Princess at the other side of the ambulance. His face was tense as he bent over his patient, but the royal mother was glowing with happiness.

He's not worrying about Princess Karine, Jacky thought as she watched the furrowed brow. The promise of a son has been fulfilled; he should be radiant! That man has so many problems . . .

And then she remembered Madeleine's letter. Guiltily, she fished it out of her pocket and said quietly.

'Madeleine asked me to give you this.'

Carl stared at it for a moment before putting it

unopened in his pocket.
   'I think it's important,' she told him gently.
   'It can wait,' was his brusque reply.

CHAPTER ELEVEN

IT SEEMED as if the entire staff of the hospital had been alerted to the fact that a royal baby was arriving. Willing hands reached inside the ambulance to take care of the Princess and her son.

'You can leave your patients in our care now,' Jim Gregory told Carl. 'I'll settle them in while you take a break. Come along in about half an hour and we'll check everything out together.'

The surgeon nodded wearily as he followed his colleague towards the glass entrance doors. Jacky, close behind her boss, thought that a break would be no bad thing. They hadn't stopped since leaving Cape Cod that morning. With a start, she realised that the man beside her was Prince George.

'I can't thank you enough for all your help, Sister,' he told her gratefully.

They had reached the wide glass doors and she turned to smile at the Prince before acknowledging his thanks. A couple of photographers were hovering by the door, and one of them reached forward to give her a slight push.

'Move aside . . . we want to get one of the Prince,' the reporter requested in a loud voice.

Jacky glared at him and put out a hand to steady herself against the door. The next second she heard a shot and felt the full weight of a body on top of her. As she hit the hard stone of the pavement she realised that the Prince too had been floored. His frightened eyes, only inches from her own, gazed upwards in terror. As she tried to move, she realised that the body on top of her was moving.

'Keep down,' ordered Carl as he spread himself over the Prince and Jacky. 'There's some maniac out there taking pot shots!'

Jacky felt a trickle of something warm on her face. She ran a finger over it. Blood! she saw in horrified surprise. Carl must have been wounded as he threw himself over them.

'Let me take a look at you,' Carl,' she began anxiously. 'You're hurt . . .'

'Stay down!' he repeated, and Jacky closed her eyes and prayed that someone would catch the gunman before very long. She hadn't realised just how heavy Carl was, and he was obviously in some pain. She was dying to investigate the extent of his injuries.

After what seemed like an eternity but was actually only a few minutes she heard a welcome voice say,

'It's OK, you can get up now. Are you all right, sir?'

Jacky opened her eyes and stared up at a tall man who was bending over them. Where have I seen him before? she found herself wondering as she noticed wisps of ginger hair. No, it can't be . . . but it is! It was the man she had seen at Niagara. There was no doubt about it as he helped her to her feet.

But there was no time to wonder about this coincidence as she was whisked inside the hospital. The Prince, looking decidedly shaken, was still beside her, but Carl had been put on a stretcher and was rapidly moving away from her.

'Carl!' she called, but the figure on the stretcher didn't move.

'Are you a relative?' one of the doctors asked, noting her obvious distress.

'No . . . he's my boss. I'm a Nursing Sister,' she began, and then everything seemed to swim round. The young doctor's face diappeared into an unrecognisable haze. His lips were moving, but she couldn't hear what he was saying as she fell towards him.

* * *

'She's still in shock—I'm not surprised, poor girl. What a terrible thing to happen!' Through the mists of consciousness Jacky could hear voices discussing a patient. It was several seconds before she realised that the patient was herself! She opened her eyes and was surprised to find that it was impossible to keep them open. The light from the corridor outside the door was shining in upon her and it seemed inordinately bright.

'Please will you put out that light,' she asked quickly. 'There's a pain in my right eye . . .'

'That's only to be expected,' said a kindly voice, and Jacky screwed up her eyes to inspect the outline of a warm friendly face above a white dress. 'We think you've got herpes zoster of the ophthalmic nerve— shingles, you know,' the nurse explained cheerfully, forgetting for the moment that her patient was a nurse herself.

'But how on earth . . .?' Jacky began, but broke off as her head started to throb.

'You must have been incubating it for some time; been a bit run down, have you?' the nurse queried gently.

'I've been working hard . . . and yes, I have felt very tired recently, but I thought . . .'Jacky stopped in embarrassment. There was no point in explaining that she had this infuriating boss and she had put her recent weariness down to the fact that she was worried about him. And also she was hopelessly infatuated with him, without a chance of ever being able to do anything about it . . .

'It often takes a shock to bring out shingles,' continued the nurse. 'Anyway, you're in the right place. Prince George has asked that you receive the best possible treatment and he's going to foot the bill. My my it must be great working for royalty!'

'But I can't stay here,' Jacky protested feebly, although as she said it she knew there was nothing she would like better than to be looked after until the awful pain disappeared from her head. 'Who's looking after my patients?' she asked quietly.

'If you mean the little Princesses—well, they're at home, and we've sent a private nurse to take care of them while you're in here. And Princess Karine is doing just fine in the Obstetrics Department. We've got the baby in the special care unit. He'll have to stay in his incubator for some time, but he's out of danger. I'm going to leave you to get some more sleep now. Press that bell if you need anything.' The nurse was beginning to close the door on her patient.

'Nurse,' Jacky called hesitantly, 'how's Dr Harvey?'

'Oh, you mean the dashing hero,' the nurse beamed. 'Wasn't he fantastic, throwing himself over the Prince like that! Saved his life—and yours too, I shouldn't wonder.'

'But how *is* he?' Jacky repeated impatiently.

The nurse hesitated. 'He's still down in surgery, I believe. They're trying to remove the bullet. I'll keep you posted; but you mustn't worry. He's got the best surgical team working on him.'

The door closed, and Jacky was plunged into almost total darkness. Through the window she could see a large crescent moon. It wasn't as beautiful as the moon she had watched with Carl at Cape Cod, she reflected. But it must be, she mused. There's only one moon . . . Oh dear; I'm rambling . . . I feel hot and my head is full of beating drums . . .

She slept fitfully throughout her first night in hospital. Carl's face kept looming up in front of her. She tried to touch it and it moved away and crumbled into a thousand pieces. Her first thought on waking in the morning was to find out how he was. The nurse had said she wasn't to worry, but it was impossible not to. Supposing he didn't survive surgery . . .

Feverishly she reached for the bell.

'How are we today?' The nurse breezed in to answer her call.

'Never mind me,' Jacky snapped. 'How's Dr Harvey? Did they get the bullet out?'

'It was lodged very close to the heart, but yes, they got it out. It had penetrated the chest wall. He's very lucky to be alive,' the nurse told her quietly.

'Can I see him?' she asked earnestly.

'No visitors except next of kin,' was the bright professional answer. 'And you're hardly that, are you? Anyway, you're in no fit state to go visiting anyone. You've got to get yourself better before we let you out of this room. Put this thermometer under your tongue.'

Jacky lay back on the pillow and submitted to being a patient. She knew by the look on the nurse's face that her temperature was too high, but she felt too weak to care.

For several days she alternated between fretful sleep and painful waking. Once she caught a glimpse of herself in a mirror as one of the young nurses swabbed her right eye. The whole of one side of her face seemed distorted with swelling, and she gasped. There was no way she would venture outside her room until the swelling had subsided, she vowed. But she continued to make enquiries about Carl and was heartened to hear that he was making good progress. There's no point in rushing things, she told herself firmly. As soon as my strength returns I'll ask if I can go and see him. After all, I owe him some thanks for saving my life.

On the first morning that she dared to examine her face in the mirror, she was pleased to see that the swelling had subsided. There was a telltale scar above her right eye, but apart from that and an unnatural pallor there was nothing to show that she had been ill. She refused her pain-killers, saying that she was better now. The pain had gone and the ophthalmic nerve seemed to have healed.

'You can't leave us yet,' the nurse told her gently. 'We have to do some tests to make sure that there's no damage to the eye. And you'll probably feel weak for some time. Why don't you just relax and enjoy the rest? It's obvious you've been overworking.'

'I'd like to go and see Dr Harvey.'

The nurse pulled a wry face at the request. 'That may not be possible, but I'll make enquiries.'

Jacky smiled for the first time in days. 'Thanks, nurse,' she murmured, and lay back amongst her pillows to await the outcome of her request. To think that Carl is somewhere here in the building, she thought happily. They can't possibly refuse me. I'm his medical assistant—his right-hand woman! She grinned at the thought and reflected that absence certainly made the heart grow fonder . . .

'Sister Diamond?'

'Yes?' she answered expectantly as a young doctor came into her room.

'I've been asked to make a full examination . . .'

'But I'm going to see Dr Harvey very soon,' Jacky began earnestly. 'Can't you examine me later? I've been waiting for so long . . .' She paused in embarrassment as the doctor stared at her.

'I realise that you're in a hurry to see your boss,' he put in evenly. 'But I've been told that you can't go along there for half an hour. Mrs Harvey is with him and he's only allowed one visitor at a time. So you see we have an excellent opportunity to . . .'

But she wasn't listening to him any longer. So Victoria had flown up to be with Carl, had she? Then the reconciliation must be complete. She stared up at the young doctor and submitted to his examination without further protest. Better get myself fit again, she thought wryly. The sooner I can fly back to the UK the better!

'You can go along to see Dr Harvey now,' the doctor

told her at the end of the examination. 'I'll ask Nurse to show you the way. But don't over-exert yourself. You're still weak and you've had a big shock. These things take time.'

If you only knew! Jacky thought grimly as she pulled herself out of bed. The nurse had returned and was fishing in the cupboard for her slippers. She glanced down at her legs as they hung over the side of the bed. They looked thin and spindly and the healthy tan she had accumulated over the summer months had dwindled into a yellow pallor. She wiggled her toes into the slippers and stood up.

'Take it easy,' the nurse told her as she put an arm round her for support. 'I think I'd better get a wheelchair—you don't look very steady on your feet.'

Jacky was glad she'd taken the nurse's advice as she was wheeled along the lengthy corridors. I would have been worn out before I got there, she thought as the nurse turned down yet another long floor. Through the windows she caught a glimpse of other tall medical buildings and marvelled at the sheer size of the Detroit Medical Center.

'Don't you get lost working in a place like this?'

The nurse smiled at Jacky's question. 'I haven't done so far. It's pretty fantastic, isn't it? There are six institutions all together on a hundred-acre site. And we're surrounded by a further one hundred and forty acres of related health agencies,' she added proudly.

'It's a good idea to house all the medical institutions in one area,' Jacky remarked.

'Your boss seems to think so. He's always asking questions about the place. Is he planning to start something similar in England?' the nurse asked.

'Not in England; in Europe . . .'

'But I thought England was in Europe.'

'I meant over on the continent of Europe. In Reichenstein, to be exact,' Jacky explained, wondering how much longer it would be before she reached the surgeon's room. The movement of the wheelchair was making her dizzy.

'And are you going with him?' the young woman asked in an interested voice.

'No, I'm not,' was Jacky's firm reply.

'But hasn't he asked you? I thought you two were part of a team or something?'

At last! The wheelchair had reached the outside of Carl's door. Jacky wished her nurse would stop the unwelcome interrogation. 'I can manage by myself now, thank you very much,' she replied dismissively.

The nurse hesitated before she leaned forward to help her patient out. 'Well, take it easy, then. I'll wait for you out here.'

'You'd better go back to your work,' Jacky put in hastily. 'I'll give you a ring when I'm ready to come back.'

'Suit yourself,' the nurse replied easily as she tapped on the door. 'Sister Diamond to see you,' sir,' she announced as she opened it.

The room seemed to spin round as Jacky entered. She paused and leaned her back against the door to steady herself. Across the room she could see Carl sitting up in bed. If I'm very careful I'll make it across there without falling, she told herself firmly.

'Jacky, you're in worse shape than I am,' he said anxiously. 'Oh, my poor girl! Come over here and let me take a look at you.'

She made a valiant effort to smile as she tottered the few yards to his bedside, where she collapsed into an armchair.

'Looks like I should have come to see you,' he smiled, and reached out his hands towards her.

She took them as if they were a lifeline, more to

steady herself than anything else. But at the touch of
those smooth tapering fingers the old magic returned
and she knew she would never be able to forget this
man. She allowed herself the luxury of gazing up into
those oh-so-familiar eyes and her toes curled up inside
her slippers. I don't need to be near him again, she told
herself firmly. We'll soon be apart for ever, but just for
these few moments I want to pretend that the future
events won't happen. I'm going to live for the present
and store up memories for the cold dark days without
him . . .

'They told me you've had herpes zoster of the
ophthalmic nerve,' Carl said quietly, still holding on to
her hands. 'I see you've got a scar above your eye.' He
moved one of his skilful hands and traced the line of her
forehead. 'Poor Jacky!'

His deep sympathetic voice opened up the floodgates
of her misery and tears began to flow down her
cheeks.

'Hey, we can't have this,' he told her gently as he
reached forward to wipe her cheeks with a large white
man-size handkerchief.

Jacky caught a waft of his cologne on the cool linen
as he dried her cheeks. 'I'm sorry; I didn't mean to
cry . . .'

'Of course you didn't. You've had a pretty tough time
and now you need building up again.' He was using his
cajoling bedside manner voice. 'Your strength is at its
lowest ebb.'

'But I'm the one who came to visit you, Carl,' she put
in hastily as she made an effort to pull herself together.
'How are you?'

He laughed at her concern. 'I'm fine. They did a great
job on me down in Surgery. A wonderful team they've
got here. They even gave me the bullet as a souvenir;
would you like to see it?'

Jacky shivered. 'No, thanks.' She certainly didn't

want to see the bullet that might have killed him! 'Do they know who fired it?' she asked quickly.

'Some crank who wanted to get rid of Prince George, apparently. He'd heard about the assembly plant he plans to open in Reichenstein to finance our medical project and thought that this would take jobs from this area. In actual fact, it will create jobs here, because the motor components will be made here in Detroit and shipped out to Reichenstein for assembly. It's going to be a massive project. I can't wait to get started on the medical side. I'm longing to get back into surgery!' Carl's eyes shone with excitement.

'But have they caught him—this maniac?' Jacky asked anxiously.

'Oh yes; the police were on to him within seconds.' He gave her a wry grin. 'Luckily I had a detective following me and he was able to apprehend the man immediately.'

'You had a detective following you?' she repeated. 'Was that the man with ginger hair who spoke to us after the assassination attempt?' A faint light was beginning to dawn.

'Yes, that was the man.' Carl was staring at her with a questioning look on his face. 'Why do you ask?'

She shifted uneasily in her chair. 'I saw him at Niagara . . .'

'You saw him at Niagara?' he burst in, and gave a faint whistle of surprise. 'Where exactly did you see him?'

She looked away from him for a second. Better come clean, she thought, and took a deep breath as she met his searching eyes. 'I happened to be looking out of my hotel window and . . . and I saw you talking to him in the garden. Then the next day, he was in the lift going down under the Falls, but you ignored each other. And I'm not sure, I could be mistaken, but I might have caught a glimpse of him on the *Maid of the Mist*.'

She paused for breath. The effort of the confession had exhausted her.

'Quite the little detective yourself, aren't you?' Carl remarked evenly. 'You're right about seeing him on the boat and the other places.'

'But why was he following you?'

'So we could compare notes about Matthew,' he explained.

'But why would you want to do that? I'm sorry, I don't quite follow . . .' Jacky began in a bewildered voice.

He smiled. 'I'm not surprised you don't understand at this stage. It's a long story. I don't know if you're strong enough to take all this in one session. Let's have some coffee to fortify ourselves.' He pressed the bell at the side of his bed and a young nurse appeared.

Jacky was trying to be patient as the coffee was poured and handed round. As the nurse departed she began her impatient questioning.

'Now what's all this about Matthew?'

Carl put a finger under her chin in the gesture that made her shiver with pent-up longing. His eyes had taken on a serious look. 'Poor Matthew had got himself mixed up in an international organisation that makes money from stealing medical secrets. They're particularly good at finding out impoverished students and offering them money in return for details of new drugs that are not yet on the market. In his student days Matthew had been a friend of Chris Douglas . . .'

'Matthew knew Chris?' Jacky repeated Carl's statement in bewilderment. 'But I had no idea . . .'

He ignored her interruption as his explanation gathered momentum. 'Matthew knew that Chris was a diabetic and he persuaded him to put himself forward to test the new insulin product. He agreed to split his fee if Chris would supply him with a sample of the substance. Unfortunately, we turned Chris down . . .'

'Because his diabetes was too mild. I remember you telling me this,' Jacky put in eagerly.

Carl hesitated. 'That was partly the reason.' He took a deep breath. 'We had also discovered that Chris Douglas was not to be trusted where new drugs were concerned. On a previous occasion when we'd used his services we suspected him of experimenting with two drugs at once to give himself a state of heightened euphoria . . .'

'That explains a lot,' she said quietly. 'I suspected he might be using drugs. His moods would swing from one extreme to the other, but when I challenged him about it he'd get angry and say that it was his wretched diabetes mellitus. If ever he caught me staring into his eyes he accused me of examing his pupils for dilation—and he was right! Oh God, it was awful, Carl; you've no idea how awful it was! For the first few days after his death I felt nothing but relief . . .'

Carl took her in his strong arms as the tears began to flow. His hands stroked her hair as he murmured, 'I understand . . .'

'But I felt so guilty! I should have felt sad, but I felt as if a millstone had been taken from around my neck.'

'So you decided to take up the millstone again in the form of your own investigation into Chris's death,' he interjected thoughtfully. 'You wanted to get rid of your feelings of guilt. And the easiest way of doing that was to transfer them on to me.'

Jacky brushed the tears from her eyes as she smiled up into Carl's sympathetic face. 'You should have been a psychiatrist,' she told him.

'It doesn't take a psychiatrist to see the obvious,' he said as he eased her gently from his arms so that he could watch her reactions. 'I'm sure that I should not explain any more in your present state . . .'

'Please, Carl tell me everything,' she begged.

'OK, if that's what you want. But don't blame me

if it upsets you.' He reached out and took her hand in
his.

As she felt the reassuring fingers close around hers
Jacky relaxed. She had to know the truth. This might be
her last chance, she realised with a pang of sadness.

'On the day he died, young Chris Douglas had
managed to get hold of our untested insulin product. He
locked himself in one of the rooms at the
pharmaceutical company headquarters and proceeded
to experiment with various combinations of drugs. His
lethal cocktail was too much for him. His body was
found next morning by the first scientist to arrive . . .'
Carl broke off as he saw Jacky's obvious distress.

'Poor Chris,' she murmured sadly. 'Please go on. I
must know all the answers. Why was this not reported in
the press?'

'Because Chris couldn't have got into the building
without the help of someone on the inside,' he replied in
a chilling voice. 'We were all under suspicion, but only
I, as director of the firm, knew that. I agreed to leave so
that the culprit would be put off guard. It had to look as
if the matter had been concluded. I was continually
shadowed and I passed on useful information as it came
to light. When the police asked me to offer Matthew a
job, to keep him under surveillance, I was dubious. It
seemed a dangerous thing to do, but they assured me
they were on to something. With my own personal
detective close at hand they assured me that nothing
could go wrong. It wasn't difficult to recruit Matthew's
services. In fact it was extremely easy.'

'Why do you say that? I mean, how did he happen to
be out here in the first place?' asked Jacky shifting her
position in the bedside chair so that she was now sitting
bolt upright. The weariness seemed to drain away from
her as the mystery unravelled. Was this what Carl had
meant when he said she could stir up more than she
bargained for? she wondered.

'The police had arranged for a plain-clothes detective to tell Matthew about my recruitment drive. They knew he'd be interested because he was still working for the international racket while pretending to do research at a university out here. They suspected that it was Matthew who'd persuaded Chris to become involved, but they had no proof until I gave it to them.' Carl paused and gave a big sigh. 'I didn't enjoy doing that at all,' he told Jacky sadly.

'Why not?'

'Because it involved someone in whom I had perfect trust . . .'

'Madeleine!' she breathed. 'Was it Madeleine?'

He nodded. 'It wasn't her fault. She couldn't help herself. It was all in the letter you gave me. Here, take a look.' He tossed the white envelope on to the counterpane.

She shook her head. 'I don't want to read it, Carl. It was meant for you. I don't think Madeleine would like me to read it.' Suddenly the idea of prying further into the sordid affair did not appeal to her. She had never liked Madeleine, but she couldn't bear to see the poor woman destroyed.

'Then I'll tell you what it says,' he persisted. 'You have a right to know. After all, you were the one who was pursuing me all the time, asking your endless questions . . .'

'I'm sorry, Carl,' she admitted quietly.

'I forgive you,' he replied with a wry grin. 'Even if you nearly drove me demented when you first came out here!'

Jacky smiled up into his eyes and liked what she saw there. This was the old boyish Carl she had first fallen in love with, she thought, and felt glad that she would remember him like this. For the rest of her life she would be able to conjure up a vision of those deep brown eyes set in that strong, rugged face. He had

lost weight, she noticed anxiously. The skin over his jaw
was taut and firm. *Now that he's solved the mystery
he'll be ready to settle down again,* she thought with a
pang of envy for the woman who had reclaimed him.

'Madeleine was an excellent secretary, but I knew
nothing about her past,' Carl continued, carefully
choosing his words. 'I had the impression that she
didn't want to discuss it, and I respected her privacy.
She was also totally trustworthy. I hadn't the slightest
suspicion of what she told me in her letter . . .
Apparently she had a child when she was a schoolgirl of
just fifteen. Her family was shocked and she was turned
out of the family home. A Catholic home sheltered her
until after the birth of her baby and then he was
adopted. You must realise the social stigma of having an
illegitimate baby in those days.'

'But why are you telling me all this?' Jacky burst in
heatedly. 'I have no interest in Madeleine's private life.
I would have thought she'd suffered enough without
dragging it all out like this.'

'Oh, she suffered all right,' he told her grimly.
'Especially when the son she'd tried to forget turned up
at her office one day and asked her for financial help to
see him through medical school . . .'

'Chris!' Jacky breathed in amazement. 'Was Chris
her son? . . . No, impossible! She wasn't old enough,
was she?'

'She'd like to hear you say that,' Carl smiled. 'Age
was one of her great hang-ups. She never would admit
it, but she was actually forty. Well, when Chris turned
up out of the blue, Madeleine was mortified. She still
remembered the old stigma of illegitimacy and she
begged Chris to keep his identity quiet. She gave him
regular payments of money to help him through college,
and in her letter she assured me that she had no idea that
he was mixed up in something sinister. But she realised
now that Chris must have had duplicate keys made from

her key-ring. She remembers lending him the whole bunch one day when he begged to borrow her car to take out a girlfriend . . .'

'Oh no!' wailed Jacky. 'I thought it was rather a smart car for a medical student. I suppose he was trying to impress me.'

Carl smiled indulgently. 'I think we'll draw a veil over that little episode. After all, we can't blame the poor boy for wanting your admiration. He must have found you highly attractive.'

Jacky turned away quickly. 'Go on,' she pleaded urgently. 'How did Madeleine come to realise that it was her keys that had admitted Chris into Chemico?'

'It was something that Matthew told her while we were away in Cape Cod. He'd started to take Madeleine out on the town occasionally, no doubt hoping that she'd be useful to him. She admits in her letter that she was flattered by his attentions. A young man, the same age as her son . . . It was when she discovered their mutual interest in Chris, one evening when Matthew's tongue had been loosened by too much alcohol, that Madeleine discovered the unpleasant truth about Chris. She'd never suspected that he might be dishonest, but now she began to think that perhaps Chris might have let himself into Chemico on that fateful night. And if so, then he must have used her keys. Her suspicions were confirmed when Matthew told her they could make a lot of money together if she would co-operate with him. Are you sure I'm not tiring you?' Carl asked gently.

'No, but I'm a little confused,' she admitted.

Carl laughed. 'I'm not surprised. I found it difficult to believe myself.

'Where is Matthew now?' Jacky asked after a short pause.

'On his way back to the UK with a couple of detectives. I had him arrested before we left for the hospital.'

'You must have worked fast!' she remarked in surprise.

'We'd been expecting something like this to happen and preparations had been made. My detective only had to make a quick phone call and the young man was apprehended immediately. I think he thought we were going to arrest him in Niagara, but we didn't have enough evidence then. He panicked when he recognised my detective on board the *Maid of the Mist*. He tried to hide from him by climbing over the side. In the end he drew attention to himself by losing his footing and falling in. As a non-swimmer he was lucky to be rescued.'

'He told me he'd been pushed from behind,' Jacky admitted sheepishly.

'And you believed him, I suppose.' A glint of amusement showed in Carl's eyes.

'I don't know what I believed. I thought that maybe . . .' She stopped and looked up at her boss, wondering how she could possibly have doubted his integrity. He was the most wonderful man in the world! And it was too late now to make amends. And he would never know how much she really loved him. Love does strange things to people, she thought sadly.

And then she remembered Julie, the young housemaid who had fallen for Matthew. 'Poor Julie,' she murmured compassionately. 'It's going to be a great shock for her.'

'She'll get over it,' Carl said philosophically. 'The girl is young and she's got all her life ahead of her. And I don't think her heart will be broken. She told me she was going back to college next term and she wants to take nursing studies.'

Jacky smiled. 'I'm glad about that. There's a lot of good in that girl.' She stirred uneasily in her chair. The mystery of Chris's death had been finally solved, she realised, but the revelations had given her no satisfaction. She wanted to forget the whole unfortunate incident. She had found out what she came for, and so the sooner she returned to England the better. There was no point in prolonging the agony of her relationship with Carl. A quick break was the easiest, she told herself as she began to pull herself out of the chair.

'You're not going, are you?' he asked. 'There are so many things I have to tell you.'

'I think I've heard enough,' she replied. The effort of standing up had sent her head spinning again, but she held on firmly to the bedside chair. 'I really am most grateful to you for explaining the mystery. I expect to be out of here in a few days, so I may not see you again . . .'

There was a tap on the door and a nurse peeped into the room.

'Mrs Harvey wonders if she could see you again for a few minutes, sir,' the young girl enquired. 'I told her you already had a visitor, but she insisted.'

CHAPTER TWELVE

A PETITE dynamo of a woman burst into the surgeon's room. 'I hope I'm not interrupting, darling, but I just had to see you again before I go. I forgot to ask you . . .' Mrs Harvey stopped in mid-sentence and stared at Jacky. 'Haven't I seen you somewhere before?' she asked with a frown.

Jacky was thinking exactly the same thing. This was quite definitely the slim figure she had glimpsed in the doorway of her house on Cape Cod. But the hair which had looked blonde from a hundred yards away was pure white. And the face, although attractive was that of a much older woman than Carl. 'I was down in Provincetown recently,' she began hesitantly.

'Let me introduce you two,' Carl put in quickly. 'Sister Jacky Diamond—Victoria Harvey, my mother.'

'Your mother! Jacky repeated in astonishment, and the shock of the revelation sent her reeling back to collapse on to the bedside chair. 'But I thought . . .'

'What did you think?' asked Carl in an amused voice.

'I thought . . . Oh, it doesn't matter now.' Jacky leaned back in the chair and looked at the older woman. So this was the mysterious Victoria Harvey!

Mrs Harvey moved to her son's bedside and stood looking across the bed at Jacky. 'I understand now where I saw you before, my dear,' she smiled. 'You were waiting for my son outside the house. I looked out of the window after he'd gone and saw you there with the two little princesses. I can't think why Carl didn't bring you in to meet me. I came back to the door to invite you, but you'd all gone, and when I telephoned the hotel the next day, they told me you'd flown back to Detroit . . .'

'Mother, what did you want to see me about?' Carl cut through the monologue in mid-flow when it seemed it might go on for ever.

'I forgot to ask you about the painting. When will you tell me . . .?'

'Hush, Mother! It's a secret,' her son interrupted hastily. 'I'll give you a ring about it.'

'Ah, I see!' Victoria glanced from Carl to Jacky and back again. Then her diminutive features creased into a beaming smile. 'Well, I must say, Carl, I certainly approve.' She reached forward and kissed her son before moving round the bed to stand in front of Jacky. 'Take care of yourself, my dear, and get well soon. As soon as you're fit to travel you must come down to see me.' And putting her arms on Jacky's shoulders she kissed her lightly on the cheek.

Jacky moved in the chair and stared after the retreating figure. 'I'm going back to England soon . . .' she began, but her voice was lost in the noise of the closing door and Mrs Harvey's call of 'Goodbye!'

Only Carl had heard Jacky's words, and as the door closed he swung his legs out of the sheets and sat on the edge of the bed glaring down at her.

'What do you mean, you're going back to England soon?' he asked angrily.

She stared up at him and a shiver of longing ran through her. He looked so infinitely desirable in his silk pyjamas. Only the hint of a bandage protruded from the neckline to indicate that he had been ill. Otherwise he looked fabulous . . . all man, she thought wistfully.

'Well, my assignment out here is finished,' she told him. 'The terms of my contract say . . .'

Who's talking about contracts!' he thundered as he put his bare feet on to the ground and raised

himself to his full height. 'Contracts don't enter into it.
I want you to stay with me. Good God, woman, I've
answered all your questions; I've told you all you need
to know about your poor misguided friend. Surely you
can trust me now!'

'I do trust you!' Jacky sprang to her feet and
the effort made her sway dangerously in front of
him.

He reached out his hands to steady her and then
folded her in his arms. They swayed together for a brief
moment, neither of them sure who was holding the
other up before Carl pulled her back with him on to the
bed. As she fell on top of him his hungry mouth found
hers and his longing kiss made her swoon deliriously,
and she forgot everything in the delicious feeling of
pent-up passion that swept over her.

Jacky moved in Carl's arms and stared up at the clinical
white of the ceiling. She struggled to a sitting position
and lay back against the hospital pillows. He reached
out a hand and tried to pull her down beside him, but
she laughingly fought him off.

'OK, if that'ss the way you want it,' he smiled as he
pulled himself up beside her among the pillows. 'But
you're not going to escape. There's something I want to
ask you.'

'And there's something I want to ask *you*,' she
countered quickly.

He groaned in mock despair. 'Always the enquiring
mind! What is it this time?'

'Why didn't you tell me your mother lived in
Provincetown? Why did you have to keep her secret? I
thought . . .'

'You thought?' he prompted.

'I thought you were sneaking off to meet a girlfriend . . . or even a wife,' she told him sheepishly.

'A wife!' he exploded. 'Why on earth did you think that?'

'It was something the Duchess said. I heard her talking about someone called Victoria Harvey who'd left you . . .' Jacky began hesitantly.

'I think I owe you an explanation.' Carl's brown eyes had become intense and serious as he cradled an arm around her. 'Are you comfortable?'

Jacky snuggled against him and nodded happily. She wasn't afraid of listening to this part of the puzzle. It couldn't affect her love for this gorgeous hunk of a man . . .

'My mother has always had an artistic temperament. I remember when I was very small she used to scream and shout at my father, but he never retaliated. He simply refused to be upset and walked calmly away from her, and this used to make her more infuriated. I loved them both and it upset me to see that they were unhappy together. I can remember wondering if it was my fault.' Carl ran a hand through his tousled black hair.

Jacky watched the well loved gesture and her heart ached for the dear little boy that he must have been.

'When I was ten my mother went away with an artist. I think they must have been having an affair for some time, because my father accepted the inevitable. He talked to me man to man for the first time and I felt grown-up. I remember he told me that we must let her go; that she would be happier with someone else— something about her creative talents having been wasted for the last few years. Again I thought that some of her unhappiness had been my fault. And I felt her rejection of my father was a rejection of me too.' Carl paused and gave a deep sigh.

'I suppose you've always been afraid of rejection since then, haven't you?' she put in softly.

He smiled at her. 'Yes, I think I have. I've never wanted to get too deeply involved until . . .'

'Finish your story,' she told him quickly as she felt his arms tighten about her. There'll be time for more lovemaking when I've fathomed the mystery of Victoria! she told herself firmly.

'My father took no steps to safeguard our finances after Mother left. He didn't realise that her lover was an unscrupulous devil. Neither did I until my father died a few years ago and I discovered that the swine had systematically milked away all the family assets. Not only that, but he'd run away with a younger woman, leaving my mother with enormous debts he'd incurred in gambling and extravagant speculation. When her creditors began to get in touch with me I went to see her. She was in a pitiful state, on the verge of a nervous breakdown. That was when I decided to take the lucrative post with the pharmaceutical firm. I paid off all her debts, but it didn't stop her breakdown. For a whole year she was in a private mental hospital. When she came out, I bought her the little house in Provincetown and hired a live-in maid. It was where she wanted to live—among the artist community and close to the sea.'

'She's a lucky woman to have a son like you,' Jacky breathed gently.

'She didn't know how to take me at first,' Carl told her carefully. 'I think she felt guilty that she'd left me as a child. And she didn't want to be reminded of what she'd done to my father. She knew she'd broken his heart. So she begged me not to visit her. She said she wanted to be alone to find herself again. But she promised to write to me when she felt strong enough to face what she'd done in the past.'

'And did she write?'

He shook his head sadly. 'No; I continued to send her regular cheques for the upkeep of the house and so on, but she didn't reply. When I found myself down there with you I didn't know what to do. I wanted to see her, to find out how she was, but at the same time I didn't want to upset her.'

'And in the end you decided to face her,' Jacky put in as she began to understand the whole scenario at last.

Carl smiled happily. 'I'm so glad I did. Because, as you saw, she's in excellent health. She told me that she'd been thinking of getting in touch with me again but didn't know if I would be annoyed after all this time. And her life is now so full and busy with her painting and her friends in the artist community.'

'Your mother has real talent,' said Jacky. 'I saw one of her paintings in the museum. That was when I decided I would like to meet Victoria Harvey.'

'Which picture was it?' asked Carl, his eyes bright with excitement.

'Why do you want to know?' she smiled.

He gave her a wry grin. 'I just happened to mention to my mother that I was planning to pop the question to a beautiful young maiden and she said she wanted to give me a painting for a wedding present.'

'A wedding present?'

'I'm sorry, darling, that was rather putting the cart before the horse, wasn't it? But you must know how I feel about you, so what's your answer?'

His lips were looming dangerously near to hers and she knew that any second he would silence her. She smiled up into his searching eyes and read her own love mirrored there. 'What was the question?' she asked.

'Don't play games with me,' he murmured. 'Will you marry me?'

'I just wanted to hear you say it, Dr Harvey,' she told him playfully. 'So that I can tell our grand-

children that their grandfather proposed to me in
a hospital bed . . . And talking of children, do you
know how the little heir to the Reichenstein throne
is?'

'All the reports are favourable. But the Prince and
his family have decided to delay their return home
until Christmas when little Prince John, Jean or
Johann—depending which language you speak—will be
two months old and fighting fit. They've taken on
temporary medical staff here in Detroit so that
we're free for a couple of months. That gives us plenty
of time for a long honeymoon. I thought maybe we
could fly down to Florida and soak up the sun. Do you
approve, Mrs Harvey?'

Jacky nodded happily. 'And we must go and see
Victoria to claim our wedding present. The picture
I admired was called "Storm on the Horizon".'

Carl laughed. 'There certainly was a storm on the
horizon that day at Cape Cod! I was furious when I
saw you standing there in the street spying on me.
I remember thinking that you were the most infuriating woman I'd ever met. But at the same time I
couldn't stop loving you . . .'

'I know the feeling,' she murmured softly as she
snuggled up against the wonderful man who was
soon to be her husband. All sorts of inconsequen-
tial details were flitting through her mind—
like where they would have the wedding, and whether
her mother would be able to take leave of absence
from school in the middle of term . . . But none
of it was of any importance now that the main
problem had been solved. The great weight of un-
necessary guilt had rolled away from her. Chris's
death, like his life, had been pure accident. Fate
had never been kind to him, but he was at peace now.
And she was free to enjoy her own life with the
surgeon royal whom she loved to distraction. The

storm on the horizon had blown away and she could envisage nothing but clear blue skies stretching to the end of time.

'You'll be such a hit with my mother,' she whispered into Carl's ear.

'It's her daughter I'm more interested in,' he replied with a wicked grin as his lips claimed hers in a long lingering kiss.

STORIES OF PASSION AND ROMANCE SPANNING FIVE CENTURIES.

CLAIM THE CROWN – *Carla Neggers*_____ £2.95
When Ashley Wakefield and her twin brother inherit a trust fund
they are swept into a whirlwind of intrigue, suspense, danger and
romance. Past events unfold when a photograph appears of Ashley
wearing her magnificent gems.

JASMINE ON THE WIND – *Mallory Dorn Hart*_____ £3.50
The destinies of two young lovers, separated by the tides of war
merge in this magnificent Saga of romance and high adventure set
against the backdrop of dazzling Medieval Spain.

A TIME TO LOVE – *Jocelyn Haley*_____ £2.50
Jessica Brogan's predictable, staid life is turned upside down when
she rescues a small boy from kidnappers. Should she encourage the
attentions of the child's gorgeous father, or is he simply acting
through a sense of gratitude?

These three new titles will be out in bookshops from January 1989.

W●RLDWIDE

Available from Boots, Martins, John Menzies, WH Smith, Woolworths and other
paperback stockists.

YOU'RE INVITED TO ACCEPT
4 DOCTOR NURSE
ROMANCES
AND A TOTE BAG
FREE!

 Doctor Nurse

Acceptance card

NO STAMP NEEDED	**Post to: Reader Service, FREEPOST, P.O. Box 236, Croydon, Surrey. CR9 9EL**

Please note readers in Southern Africa write to:
Independant Book Services P.T.Y., Postbag X3010, Randburg 2125, S. Africa

YES! Please send me 4 free Doctor Nurse Romances and my free tote bag – and reserve a Reader Service Subscription for me. If I decide to subscribe I shall receive 6 new Doctor Nurse Romances every other month as soon as they come off the presses for £7.20 together with a FREE newsletter including information on top authors and special offers, exclusively for Reader Service subscribers. There are no postage and packing charges, and I understand I may cancel or suspend my subscription at any time. If I decide not to subscribe I shall write to you within 10 days. Even if I decide not to subscribe the 4 free novels and the tote bag are mine to keep forever. I am over 18 years of age   EP44D

NAME _____
                                    (CAPITALS PLEASE)

ADDRESS _____

_____

_____ POSTCODE _____

Doctor Nurse Romances

Romance in modern medical life

Read more about the lives and loves of doctors and nurses in the fascinatingly different backgrounds of contemporary medicine. These are the three Doctor Nurse romances to look out for next month.

FLIGHT OF SURGEONS
Barbara Perkins

A HOSPITAL CALLED JACARANTH
Jenny Ashe

NURSES IN THE HOUSE
Marion Collin

Buy them from your usual paperback stockist, or write to: Mills & Boon Reader Service, P.O. Box 236, Thornton Rd, Croydon, Surrey CR9 3RU, England. Readers in Southern Africa — write to: Independent Book Services Pty, Postbag X3010, Randburg, 2125, S. Africa.

Mills & Boon
the rose of romance

Dare you resist...

Mills & Boon romances on cassette.

A WIDE RANGE OF TITLES AVAILABLE FROM
SELECTED BRANCHES OF WOOLWORTHS, W.H. SMITH,
BOOTS & ALL GOOD HIGH STREET STORES.

THE POWER, THE PASSION, AND THE PAIN.

EMPIRE – *Elaine Bissell* _____ £2.95
Sweeping from the 1920s to modern day, this is the unforgettable saga of Nan Mead. By building an empire of wealth and power she had triumphed in a man's world – yet to win the man she loves, she would sacrifice it all.

FOR RICHER OR POORER – *Ruth Alana Smith* _____ £2.50
Another compelling, witty novel by the best-selling author of 'After Midnight'. Dazzling socialite, Britt Hutton is drawn to wealthy oil tycoon, Clay Cole. Appearances, though, are not what they seem.

SOUTHERN NIGHTS – *Barbara Kaye* _____ £2.25
A tender romance of the Deep South, spanning the wider horizons of New York City. Shannon Parelli tragically loses her husband but when she finds a new lover, the path of true love does not run smooth.

These three new titles will be out in bookshops from December 1988.

W❤RLDWIDE

Available from Boots, Martins, John Menzies, WH Smith, Woolworths and other paperback stockists.